I0584516

Going Through

A Novel

Keith K. London

ATODAYSTORY PUBLISHING COMPANY

Tyler, Texas 75709

This book is a work of fiction. Names, characters, places, and incidents either are products of the author's imagination intended only to give the fiction a sense of reality and authenticity. Any resemblance to actual events or locales or persons, living or dead, is entirely coincidental.

Copyright © 2018

All rights reserved, including the right of reproduction in whole or in part in any form.

To all my Family members

Who made a way for Me

ACKNOWLEDGEMENTS

To everyone who made this book possible---to Glenda, my wonderful wife; to Nicole Edwards, my great and precise editor; and thanks to Caleb Pirtle for encouraging me to write my first novel.

CONTENTS

Preface

The influence of television, music and environment has many people living lifestyles that are not healthy and prosperous. The music that you listen to will greatly influence the person you will eventually become. The attitudes of your friends and their friends will also influence you. The places you go, and the people you encounter, will have a lot to do with the way you act. Try to learn from other people's mistakes. Pay attention to what is going on around you and learn to make good choices. Look closely at the personal lives of your friends. Stay away from negativity. Drugs and other mind-altering substances can alter your path away from the reason you were born in the first place.

PROLOGUE

Kara screamed one last time. The baby is born. My whole life flashed before me. Today I became a father, and I haven't graduated high school yet. High school is the bomb, at least it was. What the hell am I going to do with a baby? There aren't that many good jobs in Tyler, Texas. This is too much for me. I am not ready. I need to roll up a fatty and have a stiff drink. What will I tell my parents? They will be so disappointed. I hate to let them down. But the baby is here. She is a beautiful little girl. Alisha is her name. She may change my life.

Looks like I might be getting married. I wouldn't dare let some other guy raise my child. All the guys are trying to hit on Kara, but she only wants me. She wants me, and I want to go out and party. What a dilemma. Maybe I can do both. Why can't I have it all? I can go to the party and come home to my family. Yeah, that's what I will do.

I had planned on going to junior college and become a mechanic. I like to work on old school cars. My dad gave me his old Chevrolet truck, so I could learn mechanic basics. Things are looking good for me right now. Kara has that come back kind of loving, so I kept

2

going back. Now, we have a baby. I can't believe somebody will be calling me daddy.

My parents have set good examples for me to follow. Hopefully, I will be as good a father as my daddy is. When I was a kid we used to go everywhere and do everything. Once we were on the way to the vet and my puppy jumped out of the back of the truck. Daddy stopped, and I went running down the street after the dog. Maybe I will have some great moments with my little girl.

After I left the hospital, I went home to tell my parents they had a granddaughter. Uncle Jesse was parked in the driveway waiting for me. He had bad news. My parents were involved in an accident on Interstate 20. They never came home again. Uncle Jesse helped me gather my clothes and I moved in with him and his family. Somebody died, and somebody was born.

Now, every day I must medicate. I drink and get high to forget the sadness of losing my parents. I know Uncle Jesse and Aunt Jackie love me, but I still miss my parents. My cousin, Wayne, keeps me laughing. Wayne helps me keep my sanity. If he were not here, I would be in a mental institution. We go places and do things that I never imagined I would do. Wayne helped me to go through the pain of my parents' deaths. We will be graduating high school soon, and I am moving

3

back home. I haven't been there since the day my parents died.

Kara keeps talking about a wedding. The baby is walking and talking now. I love the both of them. But I don't want to give up my single lifestyle. I am a Baller...

Going Through

INTRODUCTION

My name is on a bullet. But I got a fistful of bullets with my enemies' names on them as well. Somebody will die. My baller lifestyle brought me to this point. I should have been a good husband and father. But I was not ready for that life. I had a lot of fun and made some bad choices. I am tired, but my eyes will not close and allow me to rest. Change is inevitable. This room is about to be painted with blood.

Standing on the platform of this stairway my hands sweat as my anger increases. I take one last look at the crowd as my body goes numb. A set of eyes focused on me. Melanin is standing with a group of women about ten feet from the crap table. She spotted me right away. She's shaking her head no. It's too late. Tonight, I will die or evolve into greatness.

I take the stairs upward to the loft. Walking to the middle of the loft, I position myself against the hand rail. I am directly in front of the crap table. Looking downward, I lift my foot and place it on the middle rail. My cigar is wet and half chewed. I guess 2015 will be my last year.

"Sir, would you like a drink?"

Not making any sudden moves, I relax and order a drink. I cannot get a clear shot. There is a huge ceiling fan hanging from a joist that runs from wall to wall. I feel the wind as the blade turns. A huge flat screen TV is hanging from the ceiling joist on the opposite side of the room. The volume turned up while the band takes a break.

A loud, deep, intimidating voice echoes through the shack.

"Play, got damn it."

My cousin is screaming in the headset that I am wearing.

"Kory, that's him! That's Big Tilley! Shoot him! Shoot his big butt."

"Copy that, Wayne. I got this."

The movie playing on the TV is "Tombstone." Doc Holiday is speaking.

"Why Johnny Ringo, you look like somebody just walked over your grave."

I walk back down to the stairway platform. With my guns set on full burst, I open fire at the guys behind the crap table. May God have mercy on my soul.

Tat-tat-tat, pow, pow, bang, bang, tat-tat-tat, tat-tat-tat, boom, boom, pow, pow, tat-tat-tat, tat-tat-tat, tat-tat-tat, boom.

People are running and screaming. A petite woman is hiding in the crowd peeping around the others at me. The people in front of the crap table are falling and hiding on the floor. Now, the woman is standing all alone. She looks in my eyes as she points her gun at me. We both stop shooting and lower our weapons. I don't believe it. The woman is Kara, my wife. We were surprised to see each other. Then, she smiled at me. I motion for her to get down. She follows my instructions without question.

The lights go out as my cousin and best friends come through the front door with guns blazing. A lot of guns are in this shack. All I can see is red sparks flying in the air. I jump off the platform onto the bales of hay stacked next to the stairs. The shooting stopped. I walk toward the crap table with my guns ready to shoot. A single shot fires, *pow*. Kara stands up with the smoking gun. She jumps in my arms and wraps her legs around my waist. We hug, and she gives me a kiss that would shame the devil. No questions asked. No conversation needed. With caution, we walk out of the front door of The Gambling Shack. I hold Kara close under my right arm. We slowly released until just fingers touched. Walking in opposite directions we say our goodbyes. We all leave in separate vehicles. Sometime soon we will talk about tonight's event. Until then, new beginnings.

* * * * *

My Story

I blew the stop sign at the intersection of Lake Placid and Greenbriar Road. With one eye closed and the other eye halfway open, I drive over the small bridge. Sleep driving like an overworked truck driver, I maneuver down this narrow oil top road. I'm glad my truck has a mind of its own. That is the only way I will make it home.

That party was lit, and everyone was turned up. Humm, I should turn around and go back for more. I would go, but my other eye is closing and the sun sure is bright. What time is it? I might be drunk.

This truck has done a lot of late-night creeping. The previous owner had more women than I do. I don't know how I made it this far without crashing. Am I on the right road? I should stop in front of the driveway to make sure I am at the right house.

My baby girls, Alisha and Kelsi, are playing on the far side of the front sidewalk. It looks like they are in the flower bed next to the house. Butterflies and hummingbirds are in abundance. My little girls are jumping and laughing. They are having a wonderful time. Their long beautiful hair blows in the wind as they run in circles. This is the right house. If I take it slow everything will be all right. Here goes.

Oh, my stomach. I think I'm going to be sick. I open the truck door and hold my head down. The seatbelt is tight around my neck. The cramp in my stomach is unbearable. Turning to my right, I unlatch the seatbelt. My truck is still rolling but throwing up is inevitable. Before I come to a complete stop, it's happening. *Bang*. I hit the side of the house. My body slides downward out of the driver's seat. On impact, my left hand slips from the door, and I grabbed the steering wheel with my right hand to keep from falling out of the truck. Crashing into the house, broken bricks fall on the ground and on my truck. The smell of concrete dust is in the air. The accidental acceleration increased my speed as my truck bounces off the house to the left. Searching for the brake pedal, the truck keeps going another forty feet down the driveway. My wife, Kara's SUV is parked to the left of my path. With my right shoe string wrapped around the accelerator, I reach down to take off my shoe. Rolling through the wood fence that surrounds my backyard, I use my left foot to step on the brake. My truck comes to rest against the plum tree just inside of the gate. I should have worn my boots.

The dogs squeeze by the wreckage and are now running free. My daughters run to my rescue.

"Daddy, Daddy, are you all right?"

My wife runs out of the house. Her beautiful brown face is purple with anger. With fist clinched, she walks toward me.

"You're drunk, again. But that is the norm with you. You are either drunk or high on something every time I see you. This is just a place for you to lay your head. There is no family unit. Our marriage is nonexistent. This dwelling is a house not a home. You get off work, and you don't come home until the next day. My watch has 11:41 am. It is lunch time. Why bother to even come home? You have no perception of what it is to be a responsible man. Go back where you been. Sorry, good for nothing s.o.b. Why am I wasting my life with you?"

Her voice is getting louder and louder. My daughters are crying.

"Mama, please do not make Daddy mad again."

Slowly getting out of the truck, I picked up Kelsi and hugged her and Alisha. Looking them both in the eye,

"Daddy is not mad, I promise. Don't worry, I am ok."

My wife is still yapping.

"Where your ass been all night? Why are you disrespecting me like this? Ain't nothing open all night but legs."

My baby girls hug their mother who is now standing, pointing her finger in my face about to touch my nose. Alisha pleads.

"Mama, please do not make Daddy mad."

I refrain from speaking, and my wife turns and walks toward her SUV.

"Girls, get in the car. We are going grocery shopping. Leave your drunk ass Daddy here to clean up this mess."

The girls got in the car and rolled the window down.

"Bye, Daddy. We will bring you something back from the store."

Looking at my babies and smiling, I leaned over with my head in the window.

"I love my babies."

They looked at me with teary eyes and smiled.

"We love you, too, Daddy."

The car started to roll backward, and I quickly moved my head out of the window. My wife gave me the evil eye and told me to go to hell.

* * * * *

Ain't Nothing But a Party

As I assess the damage to the house and truck, my partner in crime turns into my driveway. It's my cousin, Wayne, driving a bright red car that I have never seen before. He resembles Nino Brown. I call him 2Waynes because he has a split personality. When Wayne is sober, he has a bad attitude with no sense of reasoning. When he is high on drugs, he is calm and relaxed with a giving heart. Sometimes, I call him Nino. Parking midway in the driveway, he walks toward me shaking his head.

"Kory, kinfolk, what's going on? Looks like you got problems."

I answer with disappointment.

"Yeah Wayne, I got too full last night. I have not been this drunk in a couple of months. I wrecked my truck."

Tapping me on my shoulder and pointing at the house, Wayne vented.

"Look at the house, fool. This beautiful brown brick with white stones on the front is the talk of the community. I have never seen a window frame with gold sparkles. This house is the bomb, dawg. I know your wife is pissed."

Wayne keeps preaching and finally I respond.

"Pissed might be an understatement. I'm sure you passed her on your way here."

He laughed.

"Yeah, Kory, Kara's Infinity SUV was wide open. She smoked up this little oil top road. She blew the stop sign at Lake Placid and Greenbriar. I don't even think she saw me. But I waved at her and the girls anyway."

Wayne looks at me with his head turned slightly sideways and a slight grin on his face.

"Kory, you been through a lot today. I got something that will help you calm your nerves. Looks like you need to smoke one."

Wayne reached into his vest pocket and pulled out a leather pipe tobacco pouch.

"Let's go to the backyard patio, Kory. This is the last one, Kory."

Looking at Wayne in total agreement, we both journey to the back patio. While in the pool house, I turn on some music. Wayne sat down in one of the soft patio chairs next to the pool and rolled up a fatty. He looked at me and grinned.

"This is some of that Snoop Dawg, Kory. Bow wow wow yippy yo yippy yea."

The both of us start singing the Dre Day song. Laughing and acting crazy, I forget about the mess I have created hitting the house with my truck and staying out all night long. We were passing the smoke back and forth, and Wayne asked me a question.

"Kory, what are we drinking?"

I passed it back to him and asked him.

"Do you want a drink, cuz?"

Wayne looked at me through his tight, red eyes over his sunglasses.

"Yeah, Kory. I want something to drink."

I looked back at him with my tight, red eyes and answered.

"Before I went to the party last night, I drank all the liquor in my house. The liquor store had closed and that is how I ended up at the party," Wayne laughed.

"Kory, we need to go to the liquor store. Let's ride, big dog."

The both of us are feeling pretty good.

"Wayne, every time we get together, things get turned up. Here we go again."

We left poolside and walked past the wreckage to Wayne's car. I'm walking around Wayne's car looking at the detail, and I noticed it changes colors. It's magnificent.

"Wayne, this is a nice car. What is it?"

"Kory, this bad boy is a dream. It's a 1972 Delta 88 Oldsmobile convertible with 26-inch wheels. That Bugatti paint changes color every time you look at it."

I look at Wayne and shake my head.

"Wayne, where in the hell did you get Bugatti paint?" He laughs while looking over his sunglasses at me.

"I know people, kinfolk. Get in and let's roll."

I shook my head at Wayne. It looks comfortable.

"I want a car like this, Wayne. I yawned and laid the seat back. Wake me when we get there."

* * * * *

Policia

Wayne and I drive somewhere deep in the country. The bumpy ride woke me up. I got my hand on my gun.

"Wayne, are we going to Big Sandy?"

He answered.

"We're not going all the way to Big Sandy, but we will be pretty close, Kory."

"I haven't been to the liquor store this way in a long time. As a matter of fact, I don't ever remember being on this narrow, red dirt road."

Wayne just smiled.

"Wayne, you realize if we meet a car we may have to drive in reverse to let the car get by."

Wayne laughed.

"Yeah, I see that look on your face, Kory. You are holding on to your gun, too."

Looking around I answered.

"You darn right, Wayne. This place looks like a third-world country. The weeds and trees are so tall I can't get reception on my cell phone. Where are we going,

Wayne? Are we going to meet El Choppella? I don't know why you are laughing, Wayne. I don't see anything funny."

"Kory, relax. We are not going to meet El Choppella. We are going to meet his cousin, ha, ha, ha, ha, ha, ha, ha. We are here, Kory. Just be cool."

Wayne makes a right turn in the middle of the trees and there stands a fist full of rough-looking hombres. Everyone is strapped and speaking Spanish.

"Wayne, what is going on?"

"Kory, I told you I know people. Relax kinfolk."

Wayne got out of the car, and the guys loaded a bale of something in the trunk. We were on our way. I look at Wayne, and he is laughing so hard he almost wrecked the car.

"Wayne, the next time you meet El Choppella's cousin tell me before we get there. We need more fire power just in case something goes wrong."

Wayne finally stops laughing.

"Ok, kinfolk. I will give you a heads up next time."

"Please do because that made me nervous. Wayne, this is the first time I have ever been to Guatemala East

Texas. And when did you start speaking Spanish?" We both laughed. Suddenly, an old truck pulled across the road and blocked our path. Wayne slammed on the brakes to keep from hitting the truck. They were speaking Spanish.

"Policia, policia."

"Hell, that means the police, Wayne."

They motion for us to go back.

"What's up, Wayne?"

"Kory, the police are at the entrance of the driveway. We got to go back and unload the bale."

When we got back to where the other guys were, one of them spoke to Wayne.

"My friend. We keep for you. Come back next week, it will be here."

Wayne said something in Spanish to the guy talking.

"Kory, give me your gun. Get rid of anything you have that might get us put in jail."

"Here, take the gun, Wayne. This is all I have."

Wayne speaks to the drug dealers again.

"My friend, keep our guns, too. I will be back first chance I get."

"Let's go, Kory."

We drive back to the driveway entrance. A lot of guns are pointing at me and Wayne. The cars have different county names on them. Sheriff deputies from several different counties were waiting for us. It must be a joint task force. Their uniforms are an assortment of colors. Instructions are given to us over a loud speaker.

"Git your hands where I can see them. Git out the car. Lay on the ground with your arms and feet spread wide."

Wayne and I followed instructions with no resistance. While on the ground they put their knees on the back of our necks. We got the rough treatment. Putting us in the back seat, they bumped our heads on the doorway. Wayne could not hold his anger any longer.

"Damn it, you don't have to do us like this."

I spoke up as well. "You got us in handcuffs."

One burr-headed cop had a big wad of chewing tobacco in his mouth. He grabbed my shirt collar and spoke in my ear, tobacco juice dripping on my shirt.

"Tell Obama."

They take us back to the Smith County Jail and interrogated us half the night. Wayne and I had our story together before we got to the driveway entrance. They held us overnight on suspicious behavior. The next morning, they let us go.

Driving home from jail, Wayne was unusually quiet. Something is weighing on his mind. Turning the music down, I look in his direction.

"What is on your mind, Wayne? You are not the quiet type. Go ahead and spit it out."

He looked at me and looked away.

"Well, Kory, it is really not my business. You can live your life the way you want to. I was trying not to say anything cause you a grown man. But you asked me a question, so I will give you my thoughts. At this point in your life with a family, you need to slow your roll. You balling to the maximum, big dog. Just saying, Kinfolk. Still, you want to look at the bigger picture. You feel me?"

"Wayne, ironically, I'm sitting here looking out the window thinking the same thing. You must be high. The two of us do not agree on a lot of things but this time you are right."

"Kory, I do want to apologize to you for getting you arrested. I should have told you up front that we were going to a dope field. I should have let you make your own decision. My bad, kinfolk."

"Not to worry, Wayne. Half the police in town know me. My wife said I am irresponsible. She's right. I want to do right, but things just don't seem to work in my favor. Growth of inner self should be in my near future. My kids need me to be a good father. I keep knocking on heaven's door, and I think the door will open soon."

Wayne was speechless. He had a sad look on his face.

"But hold up, Kory. Let me tell you something I heard. I was at a domino game the other night at Skippy Jack's Gambling Shack. I took a lady with me. Her name is Davina. I needed to get out of the house for a minute. My girl is friends with Wanda, Skippy Jack's wife. Wanda's sister, Lakeisha, was there with her husband Alonzo. Alonzo has a brother that everyone calls Sly. He was the one whispering about Kara. Now Alonzo and Sly are big noise talkers. They love to threaten people. I try not to get involved in the noise-talking mess. Anyway, Alonzo and Lakeisha were playing against Sly and Wanda. Sly threatens Alonzo because he was taking too long to play. It got heated and almost became a fight between two brothers. While Alonzo was looking down at his hand, I saw Lakeisha wink her eye and smile at Sly. Sly calmed down, and everyone was cool. I am thinking Sly and Lakeisha are having sex with each other. I say that because the whole family is kind of warped. Sly mentioned the fact that he had a new love interest and Skippy Jack never caught on to Sly and Lakeisha. This is a recipe for disaster. If Sly's Kara is your Kara, you need to stay strapped. Be ready for any and everything. Be careful, watch your back, kinfolk."

* * * * *

Good Advice

We make it back to my house about 10:30 a.m. Wayne dropped me off and kept going. Nobody is home. Before we left the Smith County Jail, I called Hammer and Nail Construction Company. Mr. Hammond is a contractor that my family has been using since I was a kid. He finished another job, and we arrive at my house simultaneously. It was perfect timing. Also, if the barbeque grill is going when my family gets home it will be a plus for me. Getting the house and fence fixed plus having dinner ready should lower the stress level in my house.

Now, if I can get my truck to the shop, I am good to go. A Custom Trucker sold me this truck about eight months ago.

The contractor, Mr. Hammond, walked away from the fence he was repairing to the passenger side of my truck where I was standing. His workers continued to work on the fence.

"Kory, how are you doing, son?"

The two of us shake hands.

"Hey, Mr. Hammond. Thanks for coming on such short notice. I know you are a busy man in high demand. I really appreciate you being here."

Mr. Hammond chuckled.

"This is a nice truck, Kory. The ostrich interior has the big pimples on it. The paint is a high gloss navy blue with gold metal flakes. And you got the wide Mickey Thompson tires on the back. This bad boy is nice. It is a classic 1956 Chevy, right?"

"Thanks Mr. Hammond, and yes, it is a classic 1956."

"It looks like you had a little accident Kory. From the sound of your voice on the phone, I figured I needed to get here as soon as possible. I can fix the fence today, but my brick layer won't be here until next week. He's on another job. But we will get everything fixed for you, son."

"You know I built this house for your parents back in 1982. They were just bringing home their newborn baby from the hospital on the day I finished. They were so happy."

"So, tell me, Kory, what are you doing with your life, son?"

I shook my head and could not make eye contact with Mr. Hammond.

"Well Mr. Hammond, I have not been the man that I need to be. I have made a lot of mistakes. If I had just waited a few years before getting married I think things would have worked out better. The only thing is I didn't want anybody else to have Kara, my wife. She was a beautiful girl and still is to this day. So, the two of us ended up getting married. Plus, we had a baby in high school and I could not imagine anybody raising my child except me."

Mr. Hammond took his straw hat off and wiped his sweat with his shirt sleeve. He looked at me and shook his head before speaking.

"Son, in my day a woman wanted to be married by the age of 23. Nowadays, women put marriage off until they reach the age of thirty. Careers seem to have priority over marriage. They have babies and take them to their parents to raise. But the fact remains, at some point every woman wants to get married. And when she gets married, she wants to be loved and in love."

"It is misleading to marry someone if you are not in love with that person. You can love your kids from a distance, but do not break a woman's heart by pretending to be the man of her dreams. Her heart

27

becomes hardened, and her outlook on life can take a negative turn. She can become bitter and dangerous at the same time. Trust me, you do not want to be around when she snaps. If you are not in love with her, let her go. Also, when you get married do not be an irresponsible man."

Mr. Hammond noticed his workers were packing up.

"Ok, Kory, looks like my workers have you finished, so we will be on our way. Good luck."

"Thanks again Mr. Hammond."

The bar-b-que was cooking slow and low. Hopefully I can think of a good lie to tell Kara when she comes home. She always says I lie like a dog, so this should not be too difficult. Kara is turning into the driveway. With a big smile on my face, I run and open the newly repaired gate.

"Hey, my babies are home. Hi, Alisha. Hi, Kelsi."

My girls jump out of the car. They run and jump in my arms.

"Hi, Daddy. Daddy, you are home."

The girls are talking at the same time.

"Daddy we missed you."

I responded, "Daddy had to work all night long, so I could get the damage on the house fixed."

Kara got out of the car slowly with purse in hand. Hearing me talk to the girls, her mouth flew open and her neck started to work. Before she could call me a liar, I interrupted.

"Kara, I know you mad. I called the contractor yesterday, and he was on another job. He said he could not come here until he finished the job he was working on. He was short-handed because one of his workers was sick with a stomach virus. I volunteered to work in the sick workers place. And as you can see, we got our fence fixed today. The brick layer will be here next week."

"The baked beans and potato salad are ready. I am taking the meat off the grill right now. Let's all go inside and eat. I am starving from all of that hard work."

The girls go in the house through the back door. Kara stared at me while reaching in her purse.

"You lying bastard. You must think I am Willie Foo Foo."

I look Kara straight in the eye and try not to laugh. I don't know what is in her purse. But now is not a good time to find out. Still with her hand in her purse, she walked toward the back door and kept her eyes on me. I thought she might trip over something. I dare not to say a word. The way she walks reminds me of a military parade walking past the President of the United States.

We ate dinner, and I watched television with the kids until it was time for them to go to bed. My wife tucked the girls in bed. I was still in the family room watching television. She then came in the family room and walked by me with her hand in her robe pocket. She looks at me with red eyes and a flared nose. I think she is going to kill me. She is squinting her eyes and grinding her teeth. She speaks.

"Say something. Give me a reason."

I see her hand still in her robe pocket and say nothing. She walks out of the room while keeping her eyes focused on me. Sex might be out of the question tonight. Oh, well. My recliner is comfortable. I will get a good night's sleep.

"Good night, baby girls."

"Good night, Daddy."

* * * * *

Kory is the Man

A week later, things are starting to get back to normal. I think I'll chill and sit outside by the pool. My cell phone rings.

"Hello."

"Kory, what's up baller?

"Wayne, everything is cool. What's up with you?"

"Awww, man. Everything is everything. How are things with you and Kara?"

I stumble over my words.

"Well, Kara and I are better today than we were last week. As a matter of fact, she kissed me goodbye before she left the house today. I was really surprised. She has been acting peculiar the last day or so." Wayne is laughing.

"Kory, how in the hell did you smooth last weekend over?"

Looking past the pool at the driveway to make sure she is not driving up I told Wayne.

"Man, I told one of my best lies. It was so good I'm thinking about writing a book of lies. Pat myself on the back. Damn, I am good."

Wayne answered, "Kory, all I can say is you the man. I want to be like you when I grow up."

We both laughed, and I told Wayne, "You can read the book." Still laughing.

"Oh yeah, Kory, my pops said he has not seen you in a while."

I am glad to hear that my uncle asked about me.

"Uncle Jessie? Ok, I will stop by first chance I get. Tell Aunt Jackie I will be by very soon."

"Ok, Kory I will talk to you later."

"Ok, Wayne, see you later."

* * * * *

Kara's Plan

The burglar alarm buzzed as the back door opened.

"Kory, I brought a pizza home for dinner. I'm putting it on the island in the kitchen."

"Ok, Kara, I will eat just as soon as I find one of my old VHS tapes to watch."

"Ok, Kory. I'm going in the bedroom."

Here is one. Let's see if it plays. I'll get my pizza while the tape starts. Humm I love meat lover's pizza with ranch dressing. I need to get me a cold beer. Darn, the tape ejected. Let me see what else I can find. I used to have a couple of Freaknik tapes that I got from a guy at work. Somebody borrowed them and never brought them back. Ahh, Mike Tyson. This one should play.

The house is quiet. My baby girls are at my mother-in-law's house.

"Kara are you coming in here? What is that noise?" Shouting at the top of my voice I asked Kara, "Would you please not slam those drawers like that? The sound is vibrating through the wall. What are you looking for? I am trying to watch this old Mike Tyson fight, baby." These fights don't last long you know. Do you mind if I enjoy the short time this fight will last, Kara?"

The noise stops and moments later she walks through the house like she's on a mission. She stops in the doorway to ask a question.

"Where is the tape we recorded?"

As the Tyson fight ends, I turn my head and take a good look at her. She's standing and posing looking delicious. She's wearing the lingerie I bought her last year for Mother's Day. Her top is open down the middle. Her breasts hold it in place as the outfit clings to her in all the right places. The garter strap connects to her fish net stockings. Black is the color that seduces my mind against that beautiful golden skin of hers. I smile and answer her question.

"What tape?"

Now she's looking at me like I'm supposed to be able to read her mind.

"You know, the tape we recorded of us making love."

Hesitating to answer I said, "Ohhhhhh ... that ... tape. I'll find it for you later. But for now, come to me baby. Let me treat you like the special woman you are," in my Barry White voice. She smiles and walks slowly toward me confident that I could not resist her. She smiles and sits in the love seat adjacent but slightly to the left of my recliner. She begins to pose. Raising her legs, she pulls her knees into her chest. She points her toes toward me. She knows what I like. *Click, click*, I turn off the television and turned on some slow music. The Whispers were singing, "Get You in the Mood." She's right, I cannot resist her. Before we finish making love she screamed.

"Yes … yes … yesss, ohhhhh yes."

We make love like it is the last time we will ever make love. It is the first time she initiates the lovemaking. I loved every moment of it. When I woke up, I found the tape and put it on the dresser that she had searched through earlier. The next morning, she kissed me goodbye. We exchanged I love you as I went off to work.

* * * * *

Kara Leaves

The next day, I floated on a cloud all day long thinking about my baby. The women at work teased me about the red marks on my neck. I told them the vacuum cleaner malfunctioned, lol.

When I returned home from work that evening, the house felt different. Kara had cooked one of my favorite meals. I love baked chicken smothered with cream of mushroom. The mashed potatoes, collard greens and cornbread were so good. I sat down and ate myself to sleep.

I woke up about eight o'clock, and nobody is here but me. I get up out of my recliner and walk through the house to confirm my thoughts. No one else is in the house. What the hell? All I hear is the television playing in the family room where I just came from. A reality show is on. It's one of those shows filled with beautiful, sexy women acting crazy as hell, cussing and fighting. Let me call Kara's cell phone. She answered on the first ring, like she was expecting me to call. She didn't even say hello. So, I started the conversation.

"Kara, where you at baby?"

Her voice sounded different as she stumbled over her

words. She was upset about something. Finally, she explained.

"I left… and I'm not coming back until you change and get off drugs. You hang out at all night long. You come home drunk and high, and you are spending all the money in the checking account. We cannot even pay our bills. You are borrowing money from the kids to buy drugs, and they hate you for it. Alicia is only thirteen years old. She should not have to go to school and listen to her friends talk about you. She is so embarrassed. Do not waste your time asking me to come home. I am not coming back until God tells me to. Now tell me I am wrong. Go ahead, tell me I'm wrong, Kory."

There was a moment of silence between Kara and me. I held the phone to my ear in disbelief. She had planned the perfect escape, and I never saw it coming. She had seduced me and left me on her terms without confrontation. When she spoke, her voice trembled with sadness and frustration. I could hear her gasping to breathe as she cried through her pain. Finally, I answered.

"I didn't see this shit coming! I just be damned. You could have talked to me about it instead of just leaving. You left like you were hiding something. You got a secret? What is his name, Kara? I heard you had a lover. What the hell?"

After a while, she spoke.

"Every time we have a disagreement you accuse me of cheating. No, I don't have a lover. I could not tell you I was leaving. You would not have listened, and I would not have left. This way, the only choice you have is to change. If you want me and the girls to come home, change. I love you, but I can't live with you…not the way you are now, Kory. The person that you have turned into is not the man I fell in love with and married. Get some help Kory, and I'll come back home."

She hung up the phone. Still in shock, I stood there with the phone to my ear listening to a dial tone.

"Damn, damn, damn, damn …"

My heart is beating fast and I'm getting sick to my stomach. Never in my life have I been in this situation. I need to calm down, so I can think of a solution to my problem. So, I sat down in my recliner and poured a tall glass of scotch. I rolled up a fatty to smooth things over. I'm sure this will calm me down. It's my last one. It's not Snoop Dawg, but this is some good smoke. All the cocaine is gone. I guess this might be part of my problem.

* * * * *

Kory's Lonely Bed

My eyes are getting heavy and I cannot stop yawning. Walking through the house turning off lights I finally make it to my bedroom. If I watch television in bed that should help me fall asleep. Tonight feels exceptionally different. The last time I slept alone, I was a kid. My parents were alive living in this house. I can't live like this for the rest of my life.

Reaching for my wife, I grab her pillow and hold it tight. I miss her warm body. She likes to lay her head on my chest and wrap her legs around mine. When I get aroused, she laughs and tells me to go to sleep. Touching her face, I put my hand behind her neck. A long passionate kiss is all it takes. She loves to kiss. Darn, I miss my wife. We have been together for a long time. Surely this is not the end. Is it possible for me to change into a responsible man?

My cell phone light comes on and illuminates the whole bedroom. It's an update. Sitting on the side of the bed I watched my cell phone go through the update process. This is a bad dream. After the update finished, I called Kara. The phone went straight to voice mail.

"Kara, I'm sorry. I messed up. I haven't been the man that I should have been. I can't sleep, and I'm sitting on the side of the bed talking to myself. I am losing my damn mind. My head is throbbing, and it feels like my brain is about to explode. I have to be at work by 5 o'clock in the morning. If you call me back, I will stay at home and talk to you. We need to work out our problems. Things did not turn out the way I expected them to. Everything you said about me is true. I never expected you to leave me and take my baby girls. My body is numb, and my eyes are wide open. Nothing like this has ever happened to me before. Kara, I'm sorry."

The voice mail cut off before I could finish my message. Screaming at the top of my voice,

"Damn!"

I'm sweating bullets like I just played basketball. Disappointed, I get out of bed and make a pot of coffee.

Washing my hands, I stand in front of the bathroom mirror like I do every morning. After I finished shaving there is a noticeable difference in my skin. I put my glasses on to get a better look. Where did these dark spots come from? Years ago, my wife used to tell me I looked like one of those guys in Ebony magazine. Of course, I agreed with her. Now my teeth are twisted and loose. My baller lifestyle has changed my outer appearance. I look ten years older than I really am.

I've been doing too much smoking, drinking, snorting and late-night partying. Somewhere along the way I got off track.

* * * * *

Kory's Childhood

My dad would always say, "Mistakes are a part of life." His voice sounds loud and clear right now.

"Make your mistakes. Correct your mistakes. Learn from your mistakes and grow. Without growth, what is the point in making a mistake?"

Now I understand what he was talking about. Man, I need to talk to my Daddy right now. My baller lifestyle has caught up with me.

As a kid, I was an only child. Living in a rural area, the houses are not that close together. My parents allowed me limited mobility in my neighborhood. That was about the time I started creating characters and talking to them. My characters would sit around the dining room table and teach me about life. I had a good imagination. After dark, all I had was my computer. My computer was a means of reaching out to the world. Hacking was not as popular then as it is now. Some of the things I learned on the computer can get me jail time today. It didn't matter because I was having fun. I was screaming for attention. This occurred about the time I was entering middle school. I was way ahead of my classmates when it came to social media. My dad always said,

"An idle mind is the devil's workshop."

I guess he was right, but he's not here right now. I miss my parents. My head is hurting, and my hand is shaking.

Standing here looking in the bathroom mirror, totally dissatisfied with who I am. Tears begin to run down my face as I scream and babble uncontrollably. This emotional problem started when I was a kid. My therapist said I would grow out of it as I got older.

The *Meltdown*

> "Who the hell are you? You finally got caught up in your baller mess. Look at you. Crying like a little *biatch*. I don't recognize you at all. Ballers don't cry. You not the man right now, are you? She left your butt and took the kids...that's funny. What are you going to do now? Call all your thug buddies and tell them you need help fixing this mess? With your bad ass. Shut the hell up. She is gone. Some other guy is hitting it."

I pick up my wallet from the bathroom counter. It opens to the picture of my dad. He would be so disappointed in me. Daddy used to work at National Mattress Factory. During summer vacation from high school, I worked there, too. I remember one day I was walking pass my Daddy's workstation. I heard him singing.

"I'm making moneyyy."

He kept singing over and over until he looked up and saw me. We both laughed as I stood and watched him work. I told him,

"When I grow up, I want to be just like you."

He was appreciative but then corrected me.

"No, no son. Don't be like me. Be better than me."

I will never forget that day. What would my Daddy say if he were here today? My parents were wonderful.

Can I blame my life on someone else? No, I'm the one living this life. I am a grown man with a family of my own.

"It's on you player."

I keep saying over and over. My head feels like somebody is pounding it with a hammer. Punching the wall with my fist sends pain throughout my body… but now I'm calm. I'm thinking, maybe I do need some help. After both of my parents were killed in a car accident, people said I needed to talk to somebody. Talk to who? I don't know anybody who has lost both parents at the same time. I'm the problem solver in my house… but I can't seem to work this one out. I'm tired of crying. This is driving me crazy.

I have got to get out of this lifeless house and think about something else.

* * * * *

The Hood

Driving through the hood at night is exciting. There is no telling what you might see. It is hot outside. People are walking and talking like something just happened. It must be Neighborhood Night Out. I see some guys I know so I slow down and talk to them.

"Hey fellas, what's going on? Where is everyone going?"

"Kory, what's up, man? It's Dargan Street Block Party night."

"Oh, ok thanks."

I need to stop for a minute and visit with some of my old friends. Parking my truck on Texas College Road, I'm rolling the windows up. The passenger door opens, and two, half naked sexy females jump in.

"Hi, Kory. What you doing? We haven't seen you at the spot lately. Where you been? How much money you got? Let's go for a ride. I am feeling real freaky, Kory. We both are. You know you want to, Kory."

Saying all of this, she grabbed me between my legs and said,

"$80 dollars for the both of us. It's your birthday, Kory."

The initial shock of the two of them jumping in my truck had me reaching for my Glock 9 mm. I thought about it for a second and redirected my hand in my pocket to see if I had $80 dollars.

"Deja and Misty, I do not have $80 dollars. I left my money clip at home on the bathroom counter. I am going through an emotional time right now, and I walked out of the house without it. I hate to tell you no. But I have no choice."

As expected, they were pissed. Deja would not let it go.

"You are bullshitting, Kory. You are supposed to be a baller. Ballers always have money. Look at this truck. These seats are ostrich. My brother has a pair of cowboy boots like this seat cover. I am not stupid. This is a pretty truck. It cost a lot of money. Why you got to lie? Forget you, Kory. Broke ass wannabe baller."

They got out of my truck and went on their way.

"God, thank you for watching over me."

Common sense tells me this environment might be part of my problem. It's just now 9:00 o'clock. Maybe I'll go see Uncle Jessie. I should talk to him instead of screwing up my life more than I already have. I need to get to Uncle Jesse's house quickly.

* * * * *

Uncle Jesse's Wisdom

Uncle Jessie has always shared his wisdom of life experiences with me whenever I needed to talk to someone. I'll park my truck in the driveway. Walking up the sidewalk, I remember the times I played here as a little boy. Daddy brought me here quite often. Before I could ring the door bell, my Aunt Jackie met me at the door with open arms and words of comfort.

"Hi baby, I've been missing you."

My uncle walked up behind my aunt, and we all had a group hug. It's always good to see them.

Standing in the front yard with no shirt on, Uncle Jessie has a body like Evander Holyfield. His muscles are popping out everywhere. It runs in the family. Aunt Jackie said,

"Jessie put on a shirt. Come on in, Kory."

The three of us went in the house. Smells like something good is cooking. I think my aunt is part Creole. Aunt Jackie feeds me good every time I come over. After I finished eating, Uncle Jessie invited me to his man cave. We shoot some pool and have a heart to heart conversation.

"Rack'em up junior," Uncle Jessie said in a playful voice.

Unk shoots a pretty good stick.

"Three in the side and five in the corner combination, son."

"Uncle Jessie, I promise I'll take it easy on you. I advise you not to miss a shot, or I will run the table on you."

Now, he's laughing and I'm feeling embarrassed, to say the least. He talked and kicked my butt at the same time. Finally, he asked me,

"Son, how did you get to this point. Do you remember where things started to go wrong with your marriage?"

I thought for a minute before I answered,

"Yes, I do."

"Well Unk, you know my wife, Kara, travels a lot on her job. She's gone three or four days a month. A couple of weeks ago, she returned home from one of her trips. She was very upset about an incident that happened while she was away. I fixed her a drink, turned the television down low and allowed her a chance to calm down. We sat on the couch, and Kara explained what happened."

'When I'm in Chicago I go to lunch with a co-worker in the Chicago office named Brittney. Brittney and her husband are talking divorce. Right now, they are legally separated. Her husband came into the restaurant and found the table where we were sitting. Without saying a word, he slapped Brittney out of her chair onto the floor. The incident scared me to death.'

"Showing concern for my wife's safety I asked her,"

"Has anybody ever bothered you? Has anyone ever threatened you while you were on one of your trips? She answered with much attitude."

'If somebody bothered me, what could you do? I am miles away in another state, and you are here in Tyler.'

"Unk, she kind of caught me off guard with her answer. So, I told her,"

"Kara I can't help you if I don't know what's going on in your life. I am not a mind reader and you would have to tell me if there is a problem. Maybe you need to find you another job."

Then she said,

'I can't make the kind of money on another job that I make on this one. Besides, I make twice the money you make.'

Reminding her I said,

"Here we go again. Every time we have a conversation you have to throw money over my head and make it rain."

Standing and turning her butt toward me, she began to twerk.

'Kory, maybe I should be a stripper. You like strippers don't you, Kory?'

I raised my voice and pointed my finger at her.

"Kara, you are being a real smart ass right now. I am trying to be serious."

I took a deep breath and looked away from her. Continuing my line of questioning I asked Kara,

"Do guys flirt with you?" She laughed,

'Hahahahaha.'

She got up from the couch and walked toward the kitchen. I turned my head away from the television and looked in her direction. She's doing it again,

"Hahahahaha."

So, I asked her,

"Did I say something funny? Why are you laughing? Again,

"Hahahahaha."

Now she's laughing so hard she's holding her side. She got a bottle of water from the refrigerator. Then I told her,

"You about to piss me off."

Standing in front of the refrigerator she opened the bottle of water, took a sip and looked at me. Speaking in a sarcastic manner she said,

"You haven't seen me do anything."

"Then she slowly walked from the kitchen toward the bedroom looking in my direction like she was a bad bitch. She was not listening to anything I had to say. I heard the bedroom door close while I was still talking. I started to follow her into the bedroom and break her off something real convincing, but I'm not trying to go to jail. Instead, I got my keys…got in my truck and left the house."

The look on my uncle's face is one of disappointment. He shakes his head side to side as if he is familiar with this type of personality. He began to speak and hesitated,

"First of all, let me tell you this, Kory. A woman will forgive you for cheating. But if you are not bringing home any money, they will leave your ass. Now, let's have a seat and pour a glass of single malt. This might take a minute. You see, son, not to say that all women are bad, and I don't mean to hurt your feelings. You got big problems ... She is a cheater, and she is good at it. She's the kind of woman who will flirt with another man in your presence and convince you that it never happened. As a matter of fact, she will argue you down and cop an attitude if you don't believe her. You feel me, son? There used to be a song on the radio about this same kind of relationship. In the song, the guy saw his woman with another man. His woman told him "You dreaming, fool, wake up."

I looked at Uncle Jesse and didn't smile. He continued.

"It was funny at the time, but when you are living that mess it's not so funny. You see, son, you can worry yourself to death thinking about what your woman is doing when she is out of your sight. But she's going to do whatever the hell she wants to do. When a woman tells you that you have not seen her do anything, it is an admission of guilt. She never said I have not cheated."

"You are right, Unk. She never said I have never cheated."

"Kory, she is listening to somebody else. Somebody else has turned her against you. Plus, you also contributed to the demise of your own marriage. Remember, she left you once before. After you physically abused her the last time, she swore … this will never happen again. Then she came up with a plan to leave you…just in case. Except this time, she's the aggressor. She won the fight, and she never laid a hand on you. She put that cat on you … and when you fell asleep, she left. A classic move and well executed. Careful and precise thought went into an escape plan that you never saw coming. She thought of different scenarios in case there was a chance she might get caught. These hoes ain't loyal. She has a good job. She makes twice the money you do, and she can make it on her own. She is wayyy… ahead of you."

"If I have to make it on my own, I will, Unk. I would rather be with my family but sometimes things just don't work out."

"Do you like this scotch, son? It's a sixteen year."

I replied, "Yeah, Unk, it's pretty smooth."

"Son, look at yourself. If she leaves, are you capable of paying a mortgage and all the bills at your house by yourself?

"I don't know, Unk. It would be very hard to make ends meet."

"You never finished college. Your job could leave the country any day now and leave you hanging. You have been living off the insurance money from your parents death for some time now. You should have paid the house off, but I know you didn't."

"No, Unk, I messed up the money."

"Do not confront this woman about cheating at this point because you are not ready for the truth. You need to work on you."

"The first step to fixing your life is getting on your knees and having a heart-to-heart with God. Introduce yourself and confess all your sins. Take your time and cover everything. Don't leave anything out, and don't be in a hurry to end this prayer. When you pray, the first thing you should say is, "Lord I don't know," and the rest will come to you if you are sincere."

I replied, "Yeah, you right, Unk. I think it's time for me to head to the house, Unk."

We both stood up and hugged each other goodbye. I said,

"Thanks, Unk I appreciate your help."

As I walked down the sidewalk to my truck, Aunt Jackie stopped me.

"Wait, baby, I have something for you."

She gave me a book to read. The pages were all ruffled and worn. Somebody was reading and crying at the same time.

"Your uncle and I haven't always been deacon and deaconess. Your uncle should be preaching as much mess as the Lord brought him through. If anybody can give you advice, he can. Anyway, you read this book, and it will help you get through what you're going through."

I thanked her and got in my truck. Then I looked at the book she had given me. *Twelve Steps*, huh. I drove away slowly thinking about the things my uncle had told me. He's right. I can't do this by myself.

* * * * *

Kory Goes Through

That night, I got on my knees and prayed like I had never prayed in my life. This time it was real. I said things to God that I had never said before. It took a long time to finish because I kept stumbling over my tears, but eventually I made it to amen. When I went to bed, I tossed and turned. Eventually, I fell asleep but only to wake up with a bed soaking wet with sweat. Three a.m., four a.m., I thought about getting out of bed, putting on my clothes. I'm going to a place where night people hang out. The Bootleg Shack is a hot spot. There is always a party there, but again that's a big part of my problem. So instead of going out, I got on my knees again. I could taste the liquor in my mouth. My nostrils were wide open. I could smell dope as if I were in a room full of smokers. I need to get back … and stay back. Drying out is not a simple task. I keep talking to myself, but it helps. I looked through my bootlegged movies until I found the movie "Ray." I only watched the part where he was going through. He was in rehab, trying to get back. He had difficulty, but he did it with no medication. I can do it, too. I know I can. I'm feeling better.

It's early Saturday morning. The sun is just coming up. The fellas and I normally shoot basketball at sunrise while it's cool outside. Today, I'm not up to it. I'm not rested up yet. Just as I was starting to nod out, the phone rang.

"Kory, how you doing, son?"

"Hey, Unk, I'm ok. I was just lying in bed thinking about getting up."

My uncle, in his infinite wisdom, said,

"Son, you had a rough night, didn't you?"

I answered, "Yeah, Unk, I did. I'm not sure why because I have always been a sound sleeper. Last night was a rare, sleepless night."

My uncle laughed.

"Last night was the first of many sleepless nights, Kory. There is a struggle between evil and good taking place in your life right now. For some time, you have been doing things that are ungodly, but when you prayed and asked God to change you, he sent his angels to help you go through. It's like a tug of war. The angels want you, but evil beings don't want to let you go. You will undergo a series of tests. The ungodly things that you like will confront you. You will find yourself face to face with them and you must make the right decision. The evil beings know what you like. Ask God for

59

strength against temptation. I got to go, son. My wife has a long list of things she wants me to do around the house. But I am going to the casino with friends. I wish you well, son."

"Uncle Jessie, thanks for calling."

"I'm here for you, son, got to go."

* * * * *

Kory's First Test

I'm up and today will be better than yesterday. I feel much better after talking to Uncle Jessie. My stomach is saying bacon and eggs, but my wife didn't buy groceries before she left. Off to the store I go. The desire to become a better man is motivation for overcoming my sadness. Change is inevitable, I keep telling myself over and over again. What choice do I have? Everything that meant something to me is gone. I'm trying my best to stay focused on getting my family back.

I finally make it to the store. I'll get a grocery cart and stroll up and down the aisles of the grocery section. Every time I come in this store, I end up spending more money than I had planned on spending. My cart is half full of stuff, so I guess I'll find the items that I came here for. I'll venture over to the cold storage area and find the eggs. Placing the eggs in the basket I remembered how good eggs taste with cheese, so I got cheese, too. Only one more item to get, and I'm out of here. As I approached the meat section, where the bacon is kept, there stands a beautiful, shapely woman that I haven't seen in a long time. It appears that we both are craving the same thing. As she reaches upward to get the bacon, the black mini dress she was wearing rises inch by inch. The frigid air from the freezer made all her natural body parts stand at attention. Lawd, have mercy. My timing couldn't have been better. She was beautiful, sexy, tiny thick and about four inches short of reaching the bacon. Using my Barry White voice, speaking soft and low I told her,

"I'll get it for you."

I got us both a package of bacon.

This beautiful lady responding with gratitude,

"Thank you, I couldn't quite reach it. They should put things lower, so short people like me won't have to reach so high."

She put the bacon in her basket and then turned to see who had helped her.

"Kory!!!"

She jumped up hugged my neck and kissed me like she had really missed me. She touched me all over and with our bodies shielded from other people, she twerked and rubbed her soft body against mine. She reminded me of the intimate relationship we once shared. Pausing for a moment to whisper in my ear,

"Something just came up."

We left hurriedly forgetting why we both were in the grocery store to begin with.

Her car was closest to the front door of the store and I find myself driving down Interstate 20 to a big old king size bed. This won't take long because she is a today woman who continues to improve her process of satisfying a man. This woman is never boring and always fresh. There's no shame in her game, and she's wild and uninhibited. She always gets what she wants. She's a party girl who likes to have fun and has no sense of responsibility. Her infectious, sexual behavior is effective and contagious. She has a copyright on how to make love and drive a man crazy. She is my kind of girl. Right now, at this very moment, I will follow this freaky woman to the moon and back. Here we go!!!

Three days later, my cell phone starts ringing and ringing.

"Hello."

"Kory, son, where are you?"

I sat up in the bed and answered.

"Oh, hey Uncle Jessie, I'm spending time with a friend."

I could hear Uncle Jessie puffing his pipe.

"Son, where is your truck? I was at the auto auction Saturday and there was a truck that looked just like yours. Upon closer examination, I discovered that it is your truck. Your truck has been impounded, son. Some used car dealer was trying to buy it, but I told him it was not for sale. Son, get it together. You are not handling this break-up with your wife very well. Have you read the book your aunt gave you?"

I answered, "Not yet, Unk, but I will. I'm leaving now."

"Kory, handle your business, son, and work your steps."

I put my cell phone back on the night stand and watched this beautiful, sexy woman make her way to the bathroom. I followed close behind her. Taking a shower together I told her,

"You got the right name on you, Swirvae. You do not by chance have a website, do you?"

She hugged me and laughed.

"No Kory, I do not have a website."

We played spades and bid whist when we were not making love. Room service delivered both pizza and

Chinese food throughout the weekend. Swirvae had a bottle of massage oil in her purse. She placed the bottle in a glass of hot water. She had one hell of a grin on her face right before she poured oil in her hands. She was in complete control. I must have passed out. I do not remember anything else. She is unmistakably the best. She is the ornament on top of the Christmas tree.

Neither one of us wanted to leave the other. We enjoyed the moment knowing that it would soon be over. Is it possible she is the one? I don't know. We got out of the shower and dried each other off. She laid across the bed and kicked her heels like a little girl. I sat on the bed with my back against the headboard. With a pillow behind my head I enjoyed Swirvae. She smiled as she looked me in my eyes.

"I should be your wife, Kory. I have always loved you. You are the only man I have ever lusted after. When we were in high school you reminded me of one of those guys in Ebony Magazine. I wanted you so bad, but you were with that other girl. Where is she now? Are you still together? I'm not the wild woman I used to be. My mama tells me I need to go to church and confess my sins to the Lord. The thought crosses my mind a lot. I will make plans to go to church next Sunday. Everyone can change if they want to, Kory. First, you must recognize there is a problem with your lifestyle. Getting high makes me feel good. Being high allows me to forget about all my problems, and that's why I can't stop completely.   What do you think Kory?"

I looked at this fine sexy woman with tears in her eyes and I started to lie, but seeing how serious she was, I told her the truth.

"Yes, we are together, but it looks like we are headed to divorce court. I have made a lot of mistakes in this marriage including getting on drugs. My wife left me and took the kids. I miss my baby girls. My house is so lonely without them. I don't like the man that I have turned into. I have got to change."

Swirvae held me tight as if she never wanted to let go.

"Kory, you don't have to explain. I got a purse full of mistakes. Most people make mistakes in their twenties and by the time they reach the age of thirty, they snap out of it. Guys take a little longer. I got married a year after graduating high school. My husband never tried to change, and now he is in prison. He's a thug. Mama tells me all the time, whatever kind of woman you are that's the kind of man you will end up with.   Truth. Girls like thugs because most thugs are well endowed. They know how to stand up in it...but I got tired of getting my ass kicked for some shit that was going on in his head."

"Swirvae, you're married?"

"Yes, Kory, I'm married but he sent me a letter saying that he could get a divorce real cheap in prison if I wanted one. He's not getting out anytime soon. I need to make a decision because just like you, I'm tired of being alone."

I kept touching Swirvae all over her body. I cannot resist her curves. Then, I told her,

"Swirvae, this has been the best weekend of my life. As always, you never cease to amaze me. Come on, it's check out time. I need to pick up my truck from the city impound. It's Monday morning, and I missed another day of work."

"You drive this time, Swirvae. The city impound isn't far from the motel. Turn right at the next corner, and the city impound should be located mid-block. Pull up in the parking lot and let me out in front of the office. Stop, I'll get out right here -- Tennerson Brothers Towing and Storing."

As I opened the passenger door, I looked back at her to say goodbye. I realized we could not keep our hands off each other. Swinging my right leg out of the car, her hands cling to my arms and chest. She has a halo glow about her.

"Swirvae, thank you for putting a smile on my face, baby. You gave me three of the best days I ever had in my life."

Her journey in life to this point has been a wild roller coaster ride. There is a strong possibility that she can stay clean now that she has matured into a good woman. She knows what's real and what's fake. Everyone needs love, but I think women need it more than men do. The whisper of her voice speaking words she had only dreamed about explained.

"Kory, if things don't work out with you and your wife, come live with me. I'll take care of you. You've made some mistakes and so have I. One thing that I do know … all the positive aspects in my life came from my interaction with you. I love you, Kory. I have never said I love you to any man. You're the first."

Her lust had turned into love. She grabbed my face with both hands and kissed me passionately as we hugged and shared tears. I'm thinking the both of us need to move forward. We need each other.

"Swirvae, I love you, too, and if things don't work out with me and my wife, you will definitely see me again."

Getting out of the car, I watched her drive away. I'm wondering if I can make a relationship work. My relationship history is not that good. I have been a player for a long time.

* * * * *

Tennison Brothers Auto Salvage And Towing

Turning and walking away I decided to walk around the property and find my truck. Walking around the side of the building, a young brother greeted me. He was walking a huge Pit bulldog on a short chain. I stopped in my tracks as they walked toward me. I am not trying to get bit. With his hat leaning to one side, he spoke to me in a recognizable tone.

"What up, player? You the popo?"

I laughed and told him,

"Naw, man."

And before I could finish my sentence, he asked me another question.

"What you need? Hurry up ... Preacher will be out here in a minute."

He reached in his pants pocket and pulled out a pill bottle. He removed the top from the bottle. Then, he poured in his other hand the biggest rocks I have seen in a long time.

"These twenties, or you can get three for fifty. How many you want?"

I was reaching for my money clip when the side door to the business opened. The young brother looked at me and said,

"Play it off. Damn, that's Preacher. Act like you want to buy parts to fix your car, and he'll go away."

The older gentleman looked at us and motioned with his hand for me to come inside the building.

"Come in. The air is cool inside."

Walking up to the door, it sounds like a discussion was taking place between several people. The man called Preacher was sitting at a small card table with a checker board set up ready to play. The strong smell of coffee fills the room. Preacher was pointing his finger at the other older gentlemen. He spoke with a firm voice.

"Harvey, I am sick and tired of hearing about weave and wigs. If a woman has been ill, weave or wigs will enhance her beauty. A man cannot tell a woman what to do with her hair. Some men have control issues. They like telling women what to do."

Harvey responded.

"Awww Preacher, I tell my wife what to do all the time. When I get home from work, I tell her…lay down. Then she asks me what for? You can't do nothing."

Laughing, holding his side. Still laughing the older gentlemen directs the conversation toward me. Standing behind the counter where their college degrees and licenses were hanging, he spoke.

"Heyyyy, come on in young man. Welcome to Tennerson Brothers, we tow it and we stow it, lol. It's ok to laugh, son. We have fun all day. Life is too short to be unhappy. Find you some happiness young man."

Speaking and pointing to the other gentlemen,

"That's my brother, Preacher, at the game table. My name is Harvey. What can I do for you?"

Walking up to the counter, I took a seat on one of the bar stools.

"My name is Kory Henderson. I am here to pick up that blue, old-school truck with the gold medal flake. The one you got parked inside of your fence next to the white Cadillac."

Mr. Harvey shook my hand.

"Ohhh, you must be Thump's nephew? He said you would be coming by. Can you use them hands like Thump used to?"

Mr. Harvey did a little shadow boxing and looked at me.

"Your uncle was a bad man. He was the Golden Glove champion. We all graduated from Texas College."

"Anyway, about your truck. A fellow that calls himself Sly was here yesterday trying to buy your truck, but I wouldn't sell it to him. He is cunning, and you would not believe some of the shady things he does. That sucker will walk through the wrecking yard and take parts from several different makes and models. Then, he'll put all the parts on the same car and make it work. He owns a tote-the-note, used car dealership over on Palace Street. His cars are straight up lemons. When you take the car back, he will blame you for the car's problem. He has pulled a gun on several people. Pulling a gun and not using it will get you killed. Do not ever do that. I heard somebody say he is the devil's son. You know you never make a deal with the devil. He's got a little pimp in him, too. After I refused to sell him your truck, he copped an attitude. I stood tall and looked down on his little short rump. He decided he didn't want any of this 6'4" oak tree. So, when you meet him, avoid him."

"So, tell me one thing, Kory, how fine was the woman who made you leave your truck parked on the parking lot of a grocery store for three days? She must have been tuff as that woman I saw on Instagram. Her last name is Drayton. Preacher, what you think?"

Preacher scratching his head and laughing said,

"I think she was a rap video girl and a real rump shaker."

Mr. Preacher pointed at me and said,

"Kory, you laughing?"

I responded, "Yes sir."

Mr. Preacher continued.

"By the way, Harvey, her name is K. Drayton."

Everyone is laughing.

"Preacher, how you know who I am talking about?"

"Harvey, I am right near 72 years old. Sometimes the equipment does not work like it used to. That is when I logon. There are some young girls on there… ooowee…Anyway, I get an eye full. Then, I get really close to my wife and, and …"

We all laughed. Mr. Harvey said,

"Ok, Preacher, tell the truth and shame the devil."

With tears in our eyes, Preacher continued to talk.

"Let me tell you something, son. They call me Preacher for a reason, Kory."

Taking his glasses off holding them in his hand, he began to walk around the room like he was in the pulpit preaching. He wore his hat to the side and pulled down over one eye. He appeared to be bald. He explained,

"You see, you can't call yourself a good man if you're slipping and sliding, shucking and jiving with your shoes untied."

I looked at Preacher like he was crazy, and he responded likewise.

"What I am trying to say, son, is you are headed for a disastrous finish. You are hanging out with the wrong people. You are involved in the wrong things. The little money that you are making, you are spreading it around to the dope dealer...the liquor store and wild women. (That's shucking and jiving). You told your wife somebody stole your wallet out of your locker at the gym... but you messed it up on something else. You are not taking care of your home. (That's slipping and sliding). Your wife is paying most of the bills by herself. Your kids do not see you as much as they should. Your wife is taking on the role of husband and wife. (Your shoes untied). Where you at, player? You are about to be replaced. When you step on your shoe strings you fall to the ground, and that is your lowest point. You cannot get off the ground unless you talk to God. Confess your sinful life to God and ask him to change you into the man he wants you to be."

Harvey said, "Excuse my brother, Kory. He's telling you what he did before he started preaching. He has a testimony that is off the chain."

Preacher kept talking.

"When you get married, it is not about what you want. Sometimes what you want is what got you in trouble in the first place. I am confusing myself. The devil knows what you like, son. You failed the first test. Most people fail the first test. All hope is not lost, because you will get another chance. Now the three of us need to join hands and pray. Talk to God, son. I used to tell people to read the Bible. But there is a lot of confusion in the Bible. The best thing you can do for yourself is to develop a personal relationship with God. You can talk to God about anything. Come on, Harvey, lets pray for Kory."

After we prayed, I said, "Thank you, Mr. Preacher. I needed to hear that."

Preacher replied, "Go in peace, Kory, and work your steps."

I got in my truck and drove away from the city impound. The high that I have been on for the last three days is diminishing, and the feeling of uncertainty is draining my spirit.

'Slipping Into Darkness,' was playing on the radio. The song couldn't have been more appropriate. God is looking down from heaven allowing my life to unfold and revealing my mistakes.

* * * * *

Skippy Jacks
Gambling Shack

Returning home, I sat in my truck for a while before getting out. No need to be in a hurry because no one is here but me. My cell phone rings.

"Hello."

"Kory, what's up man? How you doing, kinfolk?"

"Wayne, man I am doing alright but I could do better."

"Kory, I am on the way to your house. You have been moping around for almost three months. It is time for you to do something else. Skippy Jack's Gambling Shack, I was telling you about it the other night. It's on and popping tonight. Tonight is masquerade night. Everyone wears a mask like you see on television. All the ballers and babes will be there. You have never seen anything like it. We will have a good time. No need to sit around the house and be sad. Things between you and Kara will work itself out. What is done is done. You can't change the past. Move forward, kinfolk."

I thought about it for a minute and replied.

"You are so right, Wayne. Ok, let me get a shower and some fresh clothes on. It will not take me long, and I will be ready when you get here. See you in a minute, Wayne."

In a short time, Wayne was in my driveway honking his horn. As I walk up the driveway, Wayne got out of the car. He wanted to get a closer look at my boots.

"Kory, I like those boots. Those bad boys are nice. What is that skin, alligator?

"Yeah, Wayne. Caiman alligator. They match my straw Fedora hat."

"You right, Kory. And that black jacket matches the black band on your hat, cuz. Too cool. Everyone will stop and check you out tonight."

We both got in the car and started on our journey to the party. Wayne is talking loud over the music.

"Kory, let me tell you about the setup. Skippy Jack's Gambling Shack is not like any place you have seen. They play three games. The first game is spades. Most of the women like to play spades. We are going early so we can check out all the women. After about three hours the spade game stops, and the domino game will start. The domino game is mostly guys who like to talk noise. They raise hell like they are going to fight but they never do. There will be a few women playing dominoes but not many. After the domino game is over, the crap game starts.

"If you do not play craps, leave the building. No two crap shooters play the game the same. They talk loud and cuss hard. There will be a fight. There is a chance somebody may get cut or shot."

"I have only seen one woman playing craps since I have been coming here. The chair on the back side of the crap table belongs to her. Do not sit in the chair. I do not know her name, but when you see her, you will know it's her. Her measurements are 36-22-38."

"Oh, my goodness, Wayne. This woman is fine."

"She is finer than fine, Kory. She appears regularly in videos with big name rappers. Her eyes are so pretty. She will steal your heart and soul. The miniskirt she wears is so short you can see her underwear when she sits down. On occasion, she will stretch her legs straight up in the air. She is very flexible. She teaches a yoga class somewhere in town."

"Wayne, you won't believe this. When I was at Texas Junior College, dance team members used to stretch in class just like you described."

"Yeah, I remember, Kory. Do not stare at her, or she will call you out. She drinks Hennessey from the bottle. Never touch her bottle. This woman cusses like a sailor and carries a razor in her bra. When the fight starts, she will be right in the middle of it. Stay away from her because she is dangerous."

"You don't have to tell me twice, Wayne. I try my best to stay away from crazy women."

"When the crap game starts, meet me at the car in a hurry. Kory, why am I telling you this?"

I look at Wayne with my eyebrows stretched upward.

"I do not know, Wayne. Why are you telling me this information?"

"Kory, I know the kind of women you like. That is why I am giving you a heads up on this woman."

I glanced out of the window while Wayne continued to drive. Humm, it is not like Wayne to give me a "heads up" on women. Humm, I wonder what he is up to. I bet he is afraid she will like me more than she likes him. That damn Wayne. My cousin and his peculiar ways. The both of us have the same taste in women. When we were in high school, we chased the same women. We even ended up at the same girl's house on a couple of occasions. Oh, well. Let's see what happens.

"Kory, when we get there, it will really surprise you. You will not believe this place. You have been passing by this place every day and never noticed it."

Now, I am excited.

"So where are we going anyway, Wayne? I thought this place was in the country somewhere. Why are you going in the opposite direction? Oh, we are going to The Big Wall Store. There are always some fine women in The Big Wall Store."

"No Kory, we are going about a quarter of a mile up the street from The Big Wall Store. Check out the wooded area on the right side of the street, Kory. The tree with orange paint on it is the entrance. Once I get passed the tree, there is a road to the left that circles to the right into the front yard. Pay attention when making this circle. Here we are, kinfolk."

"Oh, my goodness. You are right, Wayne. I pass by this place all the time. I never knew it was here."

"Kory this used to be a watermelon patch. Now, it's a hay field in the day and The Gambling Shack at night."

"What the hell? Wayne, are you kidding me? Is this the field where the guy was murdered? I think it happened back in the 1980s?"

Looking at me with sincerity he answered.

"No, Kory, this is not that field."

"Ok, Wayne. I have lived in this town my whole life, and I never knew this place was here."

"That's because you are not a gambler, Kory. This place sits on about four acres of fun, fun, fun. They are dancing in the driveway, on the porch on the grass and in between the cars. Let me find a place to park, so we can have the time of our lives."

"Wayne, you were right. I have never seen so many women in one place. They are walking in groups of five with no man. Looks like heaven."

We parked and got out of the car. As Wayne walked toward the house, I told him,

"Do not wake me up from this dream. Thanks for bringing me here, Wayne."

"Kory, if you don't want to play the games in the house, stay outside and enjoy these beautiful, sexy women. I strongly suggest you stay outside. If you leave with someone, send me a text so I will know everything is cool."

"You know what Wayne, you said a mouthful. And I will be texting you later. Have fun in the house Wayne."

The smell of fresh cut grass is in the air. A flatbed trailer is partially stacked with bales of hay. The hood is open on the truck like someone is making repairs on it. I am glad I wore my boots because I don't like wet socks.

Ladies are dressed in risque clothing. The ladies seem to be competing for best wardrobe failure. Body parts are semi exposed and tempting to a player like myself. I'm loving it. I see two women in miniskirts. The two of them stand about 5' tall. It looks like they have been doing squats. I love muscular legs on a woman. They are wearing the latest short, curly weave hairstyles. I approach them in my smoothest Barack Obama walk. My walk got their attention and my Fedora hat was leaning to the side. No woman can resist me. I got this. Now, who wants to go home with me tonight. They smile as I approach.

"Hello, beautiful ladies. How are you? My name is Kory."

"Hi Kory, my name is Short Cake, and my name is Amber." I kissed their hands as they blushed and gave me a friendly hug.

"We saw you drive up with Wayne. He has a pretty car."

Wayne walked around to the passenger side of the car.

"Amber and Short Cake, Kory is my cousin."

Amber put her finger in the belt loop of my pants.

"Do you have an old-school car like Wayne's, Kory?"

I love the way she is flirting with me.

"As a matter of fact, I have an old-school truck, Amber. I take it you like old school vehicles."

She smiles as she moves her hair from her face.

"Yeah, they seem to have bigger seats and more room inside to do whatever you want to do, Kory."

Laughing and admiring her thickness, I reached in and gave her another hug. She smiled and blushed.

"You do not waste time with small talk do you, Kory?"

Touching her small waistline and looking into her low-cut blouse, I responded.

"I know a good thing when I see it, so there is no need to waste time. So, tell me Amber, is there a chance we can take this farther? We are both adults, and I do not see the need to prolong the inevitable."

She looked down and put her hand slightly over her face.

"We should dance and have a couple of drinks first, Kory. The night is still young. I am not going anywhere without you, I promise, with your fine self."

That was just what I wanted to hear her say.

"Sounds like a winner, pretty lady. Let me get those drinks."

We drank and danced past 3 o'clock in the morning. Women seem to melt in my arms when I sing in their ear. Amber was no exception. I put my arms around her small waist and held her close to me. We danced until the morning dew and straw covered both of our shoes.

"Oh, dang something bit my right forearm and moved all the way to my fingers."

Amber replied.

"What?"

I moved her to my left side to view my arm.

"I am bleeding."

There is a female standing directly behind Amber. Amber turns around to look at my arm.

"Who is he?"

Amber took a deep breath, fell back into my arms and replied,

"Destiny, what are you doing here?"   Destiny answered,

"Bitch, why are you on the dance floor hugged up with some thug?"

Destiny stands just under 5' tall, but the knife in her hand makes her twice her size. *Swoosh*, she takes another wide swing at me with a huge knife. This time, I caught the knife hand and directed the knife back toward her. As the knife penetrated her skin, Amber screamed.

"Please don't hurt her. Nooo, I love her. Destiny, stop. Stop fighting, Destiny."

I finally get the knife away from Destiny, but she is still fighting me. I slapped her with a left back hand. She fell backward, and her short purple wig slid across the

87

wet grass. The short miniskirt she was wearing moved upward and exposed her naked body. Somebody in the crowd grabbed Destiny and restrained her.

Amber, crying, grabs me and looks me in my eye.

"Kory, forgive me for not telling you the truth. I am so sorry."

Looking in Amber's eyes I asked her,

"Are you kidding me? Are you a lesbian? She answered,

"Yes, but I like you. I had fun with you. We can build a relationship, Kory."

Pushing away from Amber,

"You know what, Amber? Your ass is crazy. Looking over my shoulder is not something I plan on doing for the rest of my life. We are done."

I took out my cell phone and called Wayne.

"Wayne, I need to go to the hospital."

Wayne spoke in a high-pitch voice.

"What the hell, Kory? I am on the way outside."

Wayne ran out of the house with his gun drawn. Helping me to the car he asked,

"Kory, who did it? I will take care of this shit right now!"

"Just get me to the hospital, Wayne. I will tell you what happened on the way."

The guy who helped me waved us off.

"I got this crazy woman, man. You guys get to the hospital and take care of that bleeding arm."

Walking to the car, I looked back at him.

"Thanks, man. I appreciate the help."

He nodded his head ok.

Wayne opened the trunk and took out a towel from his car wash bag. He wrapped my arm tightly and stopped the blood from flowing. On the way to the hospital, Wayne explained.

"Kory, man, I forgot to tell you. A lot of the women at the night spot are lesbians. I was in a hurry to get inside the house and gamble. It slipped my mind about these crazy-ass women. My bad, cuz."

"Ok, Wayne. I consider it a lesson learned. Who was the guy who helped me?"

"Oh, yeah, Kory, that was Slim Janky. If you are ever gambling and Slim Janky walks up, stop playing. If you do not stop playing, you will lose all your money. He is the cooler. You saw the movie, right? Hold up, we're here. I'll let you out at the emergency room door while I find a place to park."

"Ok, Wayne."

* * * * *

Emergency Room

Blood has saturated the towel wrapped around my arm. The nurse at the ER desk told me to come back to the examination room at once. Walking away from the desk to the examination room, a lady came in screaming.

"My baby stopped breathing! Please, help my baby! Please help my baby!"

The woman and about 6 of her family members are all crying at the same message. I was half way through the doorway. Then I stopped and let the lady and her baby enter first. Hopefully they will get to me in a few minutes, so I sat down and waited. The nurse smiled and said,

"Thank you for letting that child go first. You are next in line, I promise."

Once placed in an examination room, the nurse at the front desk came to check on me. She talked briefly with the examination nurse and the two of them switched places. The exam nurse pulled the curtain closed as she left. The check-in nurse sat me in a chair next to the exam table. She told me to put my arm on the table. She slowly unwrapped the towel careful not to cause further injury. She cleaned my arm and prepared me for the doctor. I asked her,

"What is your name?"

"My name is Precious."

I responded,

"I agree."

She laughed as her legs touched mine. Her dress was about four inches above her knee. The white stockings she was wearing kept grabbing my slacks. She took a warm towel and cleaned my face and head. Then she removed my shirt. She asked,

"What is your name?"

"Kory is my name."

Standing in front of me, she put her right knee in the chair between my legs. Precious wiped my entire right arm clean. As she wiped my arm, in my mind I undressed her. Every article of clothing is slowly removed, one piece at a time. I touched her leg to get a response. She did not say a word. Sliding my left hand up her thigh, my manhood began to rise. Suddenly, somebody pulled the curtain back and said,

"Colonoscopy?"

This slender guy a couple of inches under 7' tall is walking toward me. He asked again.

"Are you here for a colonoscopy?"

His mannerisms were feminine for a man. He had a scarf tied around his head like Little Richard. I answered,

"Naw, got damn it."

The two of them laughed. I sense the two of them have done this before. This scene was well rehearsed. I do not see a darn thing funny. He touched Precious on her shoulder.

"Remain professional, Miss Precious."

He turned around and walked from behind the curtain. Precious left the examination room, and the other nurse returned. Looks like the trick is on me. Silly rabbit.

Wayne entered the examination room shortly thereafter.

"Wayne, I'm done. Please, take me home?"

The two of us walked out of the ER to Wayne's car. I expressed my feeling.

"Man, tonight was filled with fake women living fake lives. It was just too much for one night. I have had enough. Some people cannot be true to who they really are. Some people take lifestyles seen on television to the heart. They get caught up in the negative stereotypes as being true and genuine."

Wayne looked at me like I was crazy.

"Kory, did they give you morphine or some other opioids?"

I continued to babble.

"Maybe I am talking about myself. There is a throbbing pain in my forehead. My eyes are slowly closing, and I cannot stop yawning. My bed is calling me. Tomorrow will be a better day. If not, I will never leave this house again."

Wayne looked at me and looked away.

"Kory, it is just one night in a million. You will get over it."

"No Wayne. Tonight, happened for a reason. God is trying to tell me something. But I have to go through it to understand it. Then, maybe, I can find peace."

Wayne turned into my driveway.

"Stop at the mailbox, Wayne. Looks like the box is full. The door is halfway open. I can walk from here, Wayne. Thanks for the ride, cuz."

Wayne backed out of the driveway and drove off. The sun is rising. Checking the mail, I noticed two bright yellow postcards. One card from Kelsi and another card from Alisha. My baby girls each sent me a letter. Smiling from ear to ear, I hold the mail tightly in my hand. Walking down the driveway, I opened the gate and my dogs were standing there with tails wagging. The dogs jumped on me and ran around the yard like two little kids. They made me laugh with joy.

* * * * *

Kory's Heart Attack

I unlocked the door and stepped into a quiet, lifeless house. As I walk through the house the sound of my boots walking on the hardwood flooring is all I hear. It is like falling off a tall building with my eyes open. But nobody knows I fell. Loneliness is next to death.

There are no sounds of laughter or ringing telephones echoing throughout the house. I miss the music blasting from the girls' room. A noisy house full of life and love has disappeared. Walking into the kitchen and looking in the refrigerator is déjà vu. The last time I looked in the refrigerator, it was empty.

As I recall, I left my grocery cart somewhere in the middle of the grocery store. There might be some potato chips in the pantry. I'm in luck. I will eat these then take a shower and go to bed. Closing the pantry door, red and blue lights are flashing. The police are in my driveway. Oh darn, hide the drug paraphernalia. I run through the house to check all my hiding places. The small amount that I found was about to get flushed.

Running past the bathroom mirror, I am amazed at what I see. The flashing lights are not coming from outside the house. The flashing lights are coming from inside the bathroom mirror. It is like a scene from a movie.

Emergency vehicles with flashing lights are rushing to a crime scene. The vehicles stopped on Martin Luther King Jr. Boulevard about fifty feet from the railroad track. A large crowd is gathering at the scene. EMTs are working, trying to bring somebody back to life. This is one hell of a vision. Sweat is dripping from my nose. My underarms are wet. Am I sleep walking? I have lost my damn mind. My lifestyle has me all messed up. Trying to stop using drugs is hard. A couple of years ago, I successfully stopped using drugs for a short time. It felt great to be off drugs. Being sober put me in the right frame of mind. I saw myself the way God intended me to be. It was like putting on a new pair of glasses for the first time. Months later, I relapsed and fell back into the drug scene harder than ever.

My chest is hurting, and my arm is getting stiff. I am having a heart attack. I take a deep breath and let it out slow. This procedure always helps but not this time. "God, please do not let me die!" I got to stop hanging out with Wayne, but it's not his fault. Screaming again,

"God, help me! Please, don't let me die like this!"

The emergency lights are still flashing. The EMTs are using the defibrillator. The body jumps off the ground each time the defibrillator is used. Something is buzzing in my chest. Gasping for air, I grab my chest and scream,

"No, No, No," louder each time.

There is a faint voice coming from my pocket. Putting my hand in my pocket, the sound amplified. Oh darn. I am not having a heart attack.

"Hello, who is this?"

"Hi, Daddy; hi, Daddy."

The mirror changed back to normal when I heard my two little angel voices.

"Alicia, Kelsi … How are my baby girls doing?"

Not wanting them to hear me cry, I quickly covered the phone with my hand. Then I speak,

"I miss the two of you so much. Where are you? Where is your mama? Are you safe? I have not seen the two of you in months. I will come get you right now. Alicia, what's the address?"

"Give me the phone, Kelsi."

"Daddy, do not come over or mama will call the police. The both of us are ok, Daddy. Mama turned off our cell phones, so you could not call us. She went somewhere with her new boyfriend. We finally got a chance to call you from the house phone."

The girls are crying. Taking a deep breath, I answered.

"Alicia, did you say new boyfriend? Your mama got a boyfriend?"

"Yes, Daddy. Mama has had several boyfriends since I was eight years old. She refers to it as a girl code and not to tell boys. Mama promised she would never leave you, but she lied."

The girls are arguing over the phone.

"Give it back, Alicia. Kelsi wants to talk, Daddy."

"Daddy,"

"Yes, Kelsi."

"Can we please come home? I cry every night and mama's boyfriend laughs at me."

"Kelsi, baby, Daddy will take care of that problem. Don't you girls worry about a thing."

"Daddy."

"Yes, Alicia,"

"Daddy, we will call you tomorrow, ok? We had better get off the phone."

"Ok, bye babies."

"Bye, Daddy; bye, Daddy. We love you."

"I love my little girls too."

The girls hang up.

With the phone still in my hand, I sit on the side of the bathtub and try to figure out what to do next. I don't know how to fix it. It is not a good idea to let my daughters see this bandage on my arm. My arm needs to heal so the stitches don't pull against my sleeve. I will chill for a couple of weeks before I go get my baby girls.

* * * * *

Alisha and Kelsi

Weeks later, I called Kara.

"Hello."

"Kara, how are you doing? I have not heard from you since you left. You have not returned any of my phone calls. Why not? Are you there?"

She replied,

"Hey, Kory, I am fine. I was moving away from the television."

She made a sigh of frustration.

"Kara, did you hear what I said?"

Still, she said nothing.

"Kara, I am still trying to change. But I am not there yet. Anyway, I have not seen my little girls in several months. This weekend is Labor Day weekend. I am taking my girls to Dallas to the amusement park. I would like for you to bring them over Friday evening. If you cannot bring them, I will come get them. You decide, and I will see you Friday evening. Goodbye."

Friday evening about half past six and no word from Kara. I will just sit here and finish eating this big Jucy's cheeseburger, and then I will call her.

My dogs begin to bark and jump up against my wooden gate. I get up from my chair and run to the back door. As I open the back door, my baby girls are walking toward the door. Kara followed behind them.

The dogs are jumping and running around in circles. They are just as glad to see the girls as I am. I greet my girls on the back porch. They jump in my arms.

"Daddy, Daddy! We missed you, Daddy."

Bending down on one knee,

"Hi Kelsi, I missed the both of you, too."

"Daddy! Hi, Daddy."

"Hi Alisha. How are you doing, baby?"

"I am ok Daddy. Are you ok?"

"Sure, Daddy is fine. I am so glad to see my baby girls. I love the both of you so much."

"Do not cry, Daddy, Kelsi and I are ok. It feels so good to be home."

The girls wiped my tears, and I stood up to greet Kara. The girls went inside the house.

I calmed down and looked at Kara.

"Kara, how are you? It is good to see you."

Grabbing Kara and hugging her felt good. Her arms were limp and did not hug me back. As I hugged her, she placed her right arm in between us. Kissing her is probably not a good idea. Removing my arms, she pushed me away. She pointed her finger in my face and touched my nose.

"You bastard. Do not threaten me again. You caused this separation, not me. You have not changed a bit."

In a sarcastic voice, she asked me,

"How is your arm, Kory? Did you think I would not hear about it? Well, I heard about it. What? What do you have to say now, Kory?"

She turned and walked away. The gate slammed. She cranked up her car and left. I stood speechless and watched her drive away. She burned rubber on me.

Before I opened the door to go into the house, I could hear the music playing. The sweet sounds of a noisy house have finally returned. What a welcomed sound. I closed the back door and did the George Jefferson dance. This is the moment I have been waiting for. Several months have passed. My house is full of joy once again. They are calling their friends on the telephone. Catching up on the latest news, they laugh and sing with joy. The three of us had a pillow fight. I haven't had a pillow fight since I was a kid. My mom and dad attacked me while I was on my computer. They made me go outside and play. I was eleven years old. It has been a long time since I have felt this good.

The girls stayed up all night. That night I slept like a newborn baby on the first day of life. On occasion their noise would wake me up, but I did not mind. My babies are home.

* * * * *

Fun with my Baby Girls

The next morning, we were off to Dallas. Dallas, Texas, here we come! The girls slept all the way. Entering the parking lot of Six flags over Texas, they woke up. I have never seen them so excited.

"Girls, guess what?"

"What, Daddy?"

"We have to ride all of the rides together."

Alisha looked at me with her head turned to the side like a dog. Her eyes were wide with excitement.

"What did you say, Daddy? I am thirteen years old. I am your daughter, and I know you love me. But you do not have to hold my hand, Daddy. Thank you very much."

I turned my head to the side like a dog and looked back at Alisha.

"Ohhh, Alisha that is so cute. The real reason that I must ride with the both of you is you are too short. To ride alone, you must be 48." Both of you are short just like your mother. Hahaha."

Kelsi looking up at the tall rides,

"Daddy?"

"Yes, Kelsi?"

"I do not want to ride by myself. You can ride with me."

I looked up at the tall rides the same as Kelsi. I put my hand up to block the sun.

"Ohhh, my baby girl. Today will be a good day. Come on, girls. Let the three of us have some fun."

Hours later, we needed a break.

"Girls, I am tired. These lines are too long. My feet are killing me. Let's find a soft cushioned seat so Daddy can chill for a moment."

Kelsi looks up at me and smiled.

"Yeah, Daddy, I agree. I am tired and hungry. What about you, Alisha?"

Alisha, looking around and smiling at some boy,

"What did you say?"

I laughed at my oldest child.

"Let's get a bite to eat, Alisha."

Alisha saw me looking at her checking out the boy.

"Ok, dad."

We took a seat at the picnic table to eat our lunch. Alisha sat across the table from me. Kelsi sat on the bench next to me. The girls are talking 100 miles an hour. All I can do is smile.

"This is so much fun. Girls, I am loving this. Today is a good day."

I said it in my Ice Cube voice. My daughters laughed hard. Kelsi takes her shoes off and rubs her feet.

"Daddy, my feet are sore. We should sit here for an hour or so."

I grabbed my baby girl's feet and massaged them with an ice cube in one hand.

"Well, Kelsi, you won't get an argument from your dad."

Alisha became very quiet.

"I can tell something is on your mind, Alisha. What is it?"

Alisha laughed and put her head down in a blushing manner. She raised her head and spoke.

"Dad, are you and mom getting a divorce? We were talking in class about the different generations. You and mom are millennials. Millennials are into themselves."

Alisha speaks with a look of concern. She starts to cry.

"There is a lot of information in my book if you want to read it, Daddy. My iPad is in the car. I can google the information for you. I will do it on the way home and send it to your computer. Ok, dad?"

Alisha walked around the table and hugged me. Kelsi hugged me at the same time.

"Ok, Alisha, google the information for me, and I will read it. I know I have some problems that cannot be fixed by anybody except the Lord. I promise I will make some changes in my life. Everyone makes mistakes. Somewhere along the way I got off track. Now, I am embarrassed at the way my life is going."

Kelsi raised her head off my shoulder and looked me in the eye.

"Daddy, mama has the same problems."

We sat at the picnic table for a while, and then we hit the town. We saw almost every attraction inside of Six Flags. Then we ventured to areas close to Six Flags.

We went to Hurricane Harbor. We jumped on the trampoline. We toured the bowling museum, the piano bar and shot guns. We went to a concert, toured the Dallas Cowboy, football stadium, and we saw a movie. Finally, we headed back to Tyler. My babies are fast asleep.

I wonder what life would be like if I had waited to get married. My selfish lifestyle is affecting my kids in a bad way. I do not want to screw up their lives. The long-term effect of a messed up childhood can land you in a place of disappointment. Prison or early death are possibilities. I have seen it happen too many times. Now I am faced with the same dilemma. That is not what I want for my kids. The only thing is, I like me. Go figure. Tomorrow, I will spend the day looking through the information Alisha googled for me.

Maybe the information will help me to figure things out.

* * * * *

Lovers Again

Arriving home from Dallas, me and the girls pulled up in the driveway about 10:45 p.m. Kara's SUV is parked in the driveway. What a welcomed sight. The two of us need to talk about where this relationship is going.

"Wake up, babies. We are home. Alisha, wake up. Kelsi, wake up."

Waking up slowly the girls are not talking. I walked the two of them in the house, holding Kelsi in my arms. It feels great to have my family back home again. We open the gate and are greeted by the dogs. The girls wake up momentarily to pet the dogs. I unlocked the back door, and it opened without effort.

I looked deep into Kara's eyes as she stood with her hands on the door knob. She was wearing one of my tee shirts with bare feet. She looked at the three of us.

"Hi, babies."

I replied.

"Hey, baby. It is so good to see you."

Still looking me in my eyes, she spoke.

"It is good to see you, too, Kory."

The four of us had one big group hug. The girls woke up with smiles. Still holding Kelsi in my arms, she raised her head and looked me in the eye.

"Daddy, I am so happy."

Alisha, with tears streaming down her face,

"Me, too, mom and dad."

As I ran my fingers through Kara's long black hair, she wiped my tears. Touching her neck with the palm of my hand, she leaned her head to the side and kissed my hand.

"Our family needs to heal, Kara."

Wiping Kara's tears, she nodded yes and spoke,

"Yes, we do, Kory."

Still standing on the tips of her toes, she spoke with joy in her heart.

"Kory, let's put the girls to bed."

The girls jumped up and down on the bed. Kelsi was having a good time.

"We jumped on the trampoline today, mama."

Kara laughed.

"You did? Did you have a good time with Daddy?

Alisha answered.

"Yes, mama. We had a great time. We rode almost all the rides and had a good lunch. We drove all over the place. Today was a good day, mama."

Kara and I put the girls in bed.

She grabbed me by the hand.

"Let's go to the bedroom, Kory. We have some catching up to do."

She locked the bedroom door behind us. She then pushed me into the shower that was already running. She lathered a small towel with soap. She gave me a bath like you would a small child.

"Ohhh, this is great, Kara. This reminds me of when we first got married. We took turns bathing each other. Those were the best times of our lives."

She got a towel and dried me off.

"Yes, I remember, Kory. You used to chase me around the house naked. You slapped me on my butt with every step. That was so much fun. Come on to bed. You are dry now."

Kara placed her feet on top of mine, and we walked into the bedroom together.

"Is that a gun in your pocket, Kory?"

I laughed.

"Yeah, baby. A twelve gauge."

We laughed. Standing on the side of the bed, Kara turned around and gave me a big kiss. We embraced for a long time. It was very comforting.

"Kory, stop sniffing me like a dog. You always do that."

"Yeah I do Kara. But your natural fragrance is such a turn on. I love the way you smell without the Chanel No. 5 you normally wear. There is no comparison."

She smiled,

"Yeah, I know you like it, Kory. Keep sniffing like a dog."

I growled at her like a dog. She crawls onto the bed on all four. She leaned back against the headboard laughing and placed a pillow behind her head.

I turned on some soft music. Sitting on the side of the bed, we talked and reminisced about our high school days. We missed each other. She pulled her knees up to her chest and pointed her toes toward me. She took her feet and stroked me from the top of my head and stopped about six inches below my stomach. For the next couple of hours, the world stopped turning. Nothing mattered except the passion we had for each other.

In the wee hours of Sunday morning, we made love. We took our time and made sure we both were satisfied. There was no need to be in a hurry. I fell asleep and woke later still on top of her. Then, we made love again. The bed was soaking wet with sweat. About half past 4:00 a.m., the both of us sit up in the bed. We look at each other in amazement. Kara turned on the television. Putting the remote back on the nightstand, she looked at me.

"Did we just make love all night long?"

Nodding my head, I answered.

"I think we did. We still got it."

She laid her head on my chest.

"Yes, we still got it Kory Henderson. And we will always have it."

"Kory, even if the two of us are not together, nothing will change. You were my first love. You took my virginity. I love you Kory, and I know you love me. But the two of us or not marriage material. Why are you laughing, Kory?"

"I am not laughing Kara."

"The hell you're not, Kory. Did I say something funny? You are about to piss me off, Kory Henderson."

She punched me in my chest.

"Kara, ok, I am laughing. Let me tell you why. What you just said about us being married, I was thinking the same exact thing. But I did not know how to say it without hurting your feelings. Lord knows I do not want to make you unhappy. But you just spit it out like you were singing along with the radio."

"Kara, it is still amazing to me how much we think alike. Now, who is laughing?"

Pulling the sheet over her head, she laughed.

"You still have a lot of player in you, Kory. I admit I still turn up a little too often."

With eyes and mouth wide open, I looked at Kara.

115

"Kara, is this a confession? Has the world stop turning? I have never seen you be so honest."

Exhaling she replied,

"Yeah, Kory, I know, but I am trying to change. But I am not there yet. How are we going to tell the girls? They are so happy right now. I do not want to break their little hearts."

Shaking my head in agreement,

"Yeah, Kara, I was thinking the same thing."

Kara sat up in the bed and straddled me. She grabbed me by the face with both hands. Pulling me close to her, our noses almost touching.

"Kory, I know I have not been around much these last few months. Not knowing what would happen with us from day to day was so nerve wracking. I needed to work out some things that were going on in my head. Many nights, I dreamed of putting a gun to your head and pulling the trigger. Yeah Kory, I bought a gun."

My eyes almost popped out of my head.

"Kara. You got a gun? Is it that bad?"

I looked down at my hands. My heart is beating faster. Sweat is beading up on my forehead.

"Am I the kind of guy who rules over his woman? Maybe years ago, I was that kind of guy. But not now. Kara, I am so sorry. Our marriage is ruined because of me. The blame is all on me. My head was in the streets. I should have been at home with my family."

"Stop crying, Kory. We have been together for a long time. I will not just disappear from your life like we never had anything real. I promise to come by and check on you on a regular basis. And our daughters can visit you as much as they want to. They need to see their dad on a regular basis. Daddy daughter relationship is something I did not have when I was a little girl. My daughters will not miss out on that life like I did."

"Right now, there is a wall built around me. I will not allow another person a chance to touch my heart. Kory, if you should find another, invite me to the wedding. I will cheer you on."

Sunday morning, Kara and I pulled it together for the girls. We were a family again. We played video games and had pillow fights. It was fun going outside looking at butterflies. Kelsi knows every species of butterfly in the flowerbed.

Alisha walked between Kara, and me. She looked up at me, and then she looked up at Kara.

"Mom and dad. Can we sit down on the front porch steps, please?"

I sat down next to Kara, and Alisha stood in front of us.

"Mom and Dad, it didn't work, did it? I am not stupid. I heard there is an old saying that opposites attract. The two of you are too much alike."

Kara pulled Alisha in between the two of us. She whispered to Alisha.

"My little girl is growing up. We cannot fool you, can we? I still love your Daddy, baby."

Alisha interrupted.

"You love him, but the two of you cannot live together. Is that what you are saying, mom?"

Kelsi walked up with a butterfly in her hand. She heard Alisha speaking. She cried.

"We are not moving back home, mama?"

I picked up Kelsi and put her on my lap.

"Kelsi, this will always be your house. Mom and dad just need some space. Anytime you want to come home, call me. I will drop everything and come get you. I promise."

* * * * *

Kory's Mental Awakening

After Kara and the girls left, I looked at the information Alisha had googled for me. Just like she said, Kara and I are too much alike. One of us needs to change. Note to self, *Change*. The next five days, all I did was work and come home. No clubbing and no partying. I tried to stay positive. Keeping the negativity out of your life is hard when that is all you know. Maybe I got this baller lifestyle all wrong. Emotional abuse of a woman is just as damaging as physical abuse. My oldest daughter is more conscious of who I am than me. I could tell Alisha was hurting inside. Little girls love Daddy. I am a big influence on the man she chooses to live the rest of her life with. I must raise the bar in my life.

* * * * *

Wayne to the Rescue

Friday after work I decide to chill and not go out. The brisket is on the bar-b-que grill wrapped in foil. The hickory, pecan and red oak wood is smoking like a train. Smells so good. The doorbell rings and there is constant knocking at my front door.

"Kinfolk, open up."

When I opened the door, there stands Wayne.

"Kory, what's up kinfolk?

"Hey, come on in, Wayne."

I unlock the screen door, so everyone can enter.

"I brought some friends with me, Kory. Everyone this is my cousin, Kory."

The women respond.

"Hi, Kory; hey, sexy."

Wayne entered the house first. He placed several sacks on the dining table. Then he turned around and introduced the women.

"Kory, this is Bambi, Toni, Crush and Melanin."

"Hello, ladies. Welcome to my home."

"By the way, Kory, do not believe anything they say. They all lie like a dog. Just so you know, kinfolk. I do not want you to get caught up in some bull stuff. It's all about the money."

We all laugh.

"Thanks for the warning, Wayne."

"Kory, you have a nice house."

"Thank you, Crush. So, did your parents name you Crush?

She laughed as she looked down at her magnificent body. She did a little turn around move like she was a runway model.

"Maybe you will find out, Kory. Today is Friday. Time to turn up. Open the liquor, Wayne."

"Ok, let me finish rolling up this Snoop Dawg."

Melanin and Bambi were checking out the family pictures.

"You have a beautiful family, Kory."

"Thanks, Melanin. I love your dimples."

Melanin, blushed. Bambi picked up my wife's picture from the shelf.   She turns and looks in my direction.

"So where is the wife, Kory?"

I looked over my glasses at her.

"Well, she is not here right now. The two of us are on a break."

Toni sat at the dining room table. She replied.

"Oh, I am sorry, Kory. Bambi, get out of Kory's business."

Wayne interrupted,

"He could probably use some cheering up. Don't you think, girls?"

Everyone responded yes. Wayne poured drinks while talking to the women.

"Toni, I am glad you straightened out Bambi. I was trying not to say the wrong thing."

Wayne looked around the table at the women.

"Why are you all still dressed? Put your bikinis on so we can get in the pool. Find you a room and change clothes."

Crush is standing next to Wayne as he pours shots of Patron. She drinks two shots in a row. She looks at me and smiles.

"Kory, I am a grown woman, and there is no shame in my game. Help me unfasten my bra, please? I am in the mood to party. Will you help me remove these tight shorts, Kory, please? I cannot do it by myself. It's your birthday."

I was trying not to act overly excited.

"Hell yeah, I will help you. Come over here next to me, Crush. I need to sit down. Let me unbutton these orange shorts. These bad boys are tight. This is like peeling a soft, beautiful orange. The juice squirted in my face. That's what the players say."

Crush put her hand under my chin and pushed my head backward.

"Allow me to lick the juice off, Kory. Players like that. Tastes sooo good."

"Yes, it does Crush. Slowly but surely, I will get them off. Oh, my goodness. You are not wearing underwear. I must get on my knees to make sure the shorts slide down even to the floor."

Everyone laughed.   The other girls surrounded me wanting to be next.

"I will take all of your shorts off if it kills me. Today is Kory Day."

The women fill their glasses and make a toast.

"Kory Day!"

These beautiful females allowed me to put their swimsuits on, one by one. We all went outside to the swimming pool, and the party started. The music was bumping loud and strong, 'Do You Think I'm a Nasty Girl?'   The women twerked and stripped all their clothes off.   Wayne laughed until his side hurt.   He walked over and took a seat in the lounge chair next to mine.

"Kory, I thought you could use some cheering up. My lady friends were all too eager to come along. We were going to the Freaknik at Padre Island. I think this is better. What do you think, Kory?"

I sit up in my seat and look at Wayne like he was crazy.

"Wayne, do I really need to answer that question?"

I shook hands with Wayne.

"Thanks, cuz. Now pass the Snoop Dawg. Stop hogging it."

The girls were all over the two of us. Bambi, with her long legs stepped over my lawn chair and straddled me. She is warm and wet.

"Do you like that, Kory? I am a nasty girl. Close your eyes, Kory, and I will take you on a trip. You know, scientists have discovered a new planet. Discover it with me. Strap in, Kory. Here we go."

Wayne coached Bambi while laughing. The other girls cheered us on.

"Work it, Bambi. Work it. Go, Bambi. Go, Bambi. Go, Bambi. Go, Bambi."

She did her special thing and put me to sleep.

Pow, pow, pow, pow.

"Wake up, Kory! Get down! Get on the ground, Kory!"

pow, pow, pow, pow.

"Wayne, what the hell?"

"Somebody is shooting, Kory. There is a car in the driveway behind mine."

pow, pow, pow, pow.

"Everyone get down. Damn, my gun is in the house. Somebody is walking toward the fence Wayne. Y'all be still."

pow, pow, bang, bang, bang.

"Somebody else is shooting. The car cranked up and left.

"Kory, Kory, are you all right?

"Mordell, is that you?"

"Yeah, me and Erik. We heard the shooting and came to check on you."

"We are in the backyard man. Come on in. Everyone, it is ok. Everyone these are my homeboys from up the street."

"Kory, what is going on?"

"Erik, man, thank the both of you for coming. I do not know. Come around to the other side of the pool. Did the two of you see who was shooting at us?"

Mordell, looking around, replied, "Kory, all we saw was the fire coming out of his gun."

"Toni, Bambi, Melanin and Crush, are you all ok? Everyone answered.

"I think so. We are ok. Thanks for asking."

"Wayne, help me get all of this illegal stuff put up in case the police show up."

"Yeah, you right, Kory. Let's get the place cleaned up."

Eric shaking his head no at Kory.

"You know damn well the police are not coming out here in the country."

Agreeing with Erik, I reply,

"I know you right, Erik. Thanks for saving our lives. I cannot imagine who would shoot at me. This is unbelievable."

Eric stood watch while we cleaned up. Less than an hour later,

"Everyone take cover. A car just pulled up in the driveway. Somebody is walking toward the fence."

Mordell and Erik point their guns at the fence.

"Kory, Kory, where are you?"

"Kara, is that you?"

"I am coming in the backyard."

Walking toward the gate to meet Kara, Bambi runs pass me. Kara and Bambi embrace and cry like they haven't seen each other for a long time. Bambi runs out of the gate, and I hear Kara's car door close.

"Kara, do you know Bambi?"

"Yes, we are friends, Kory. She called me and said she was in trouble and that somebody was shooting at Kory?"

Looking at Kara in disbelief,

"Yeah, Kara. Somebody was shooting. You should have passed a fast-moving car on the way here."

She responded,

"No, I didn't see anybody, Kory. I am leaving before the police come."

Kara opened the gate and walked up the driveway. Not knowing I was following her she got in the car and embraced Bambi again. I stood in front of her SUV and the two of them kissed long and passionately. Bambi saw me looking and told Kara. Kara turned and looked me in the eye. I was in shock. My chest started to hurt.

I grabbed my chest and slowly fell to my knees. Kara was embarrassed. She got out of the car and ran to me. Kara screams.

"Kory, it is not your fault! No, Kory! I am sorry. Please do not do this. Breathe, Kory, breathe!"

Kara held me in her arms, and I replied.

"Did I do this? Did I cause you to go to a woman, Kara? My chest, Kara."

"Nooo Kory, nooo!! Stay with me. Stay with me, Kory! Don't die, Kory, please don't die!!"

Wayne is screaming and beating me in my chest.

"Breathe, Kory."

I hear the siren, and the lights are flashing.

"Lord, I do not want to die. Please give me another chance."

"Kory, Kory, it's Kara. The EMTs are here. He is unconscious. Over here. Over here. He is still breathing."

"Ma'am, sir, please stand back. Everyone stand clear. Give me the paddles. Turn it up higher. Ok, we got a heartbeat. Let's get him to the hospital."

"Kara, what happened? Kory, Kory, Kory. Kory, this is Wayne. You will be ok. It's ok, man. Girls, get in the car. We will follow the ambulance to the hospital. Hang on, Kory."

* * * * *

Wayne Confronts Kara

"Toni, look in the glove box and hand me the handicap placard. My Daddy keeps one in my car in case he needs to use it. I don't see a parking space anywhere in this parking lot."

Melanin responds from the back seat.

"There is a car backing out on the next aisle, Wayne. Slow down, Wayne."

"Ok. I'm nervous, Melanin. Sorry, I didn't mean to scare you. Let's go inside to the ER desk. Let me talk to the nurse. Nurse, the ambulance just brought my cousin in. His name is Kory Henderson."

Nurse responds,

"Yes, he is being treated now. Please have a seat, and I will call you when you can go back and see him."

"Ok, thanks ma'am.

"We have been in this waiting room for two hours. Somebody needs to tell me something. Melanin, I will take you, Crush and Toni home in a minute. I need to make sure Kory is ok."

Melanin replied,

"We are ok, Wayne. Check on your cousin."

"Let me go back to the nurse's desk and find out what is going on."

Toni responds,

"Calm down, Wayne, before *you* have a heart attack."

"Nurse, can you tell me anything about Kory Henderson yet?"

Nurse responds,

"I will go and check on him for you."

A few minutes later, the nurse returns.

"Sir, I spoke with the doctor, and your cousin will be staying overnight for observation. The doctor will talk to you in a few minutes. Just have a seat."

I sit on the edge of my seat next to Kara.

"Kara, tell me what happened to Kory."

Kara looks at me and is speechless.

"Kara, got damn it! What happened to my cousin?"

Kara looked at me and looked down.

"Kory saw Bambi in my car. I hugged Bambi and when I turned around Kory was sliding down the hood of my car."

Grabbing Kara by her face, I turned her toward me.

"No shit? Kory saw you and Bambi hugging. Is that all?"

Kara nods her head yes.

"Kara, I know people who know you. I have seen pictures and videos of you with guys and girls at the same time. I was hoping you would change. We all got skeletons in our closet. But it looks like you need a bigger closet. Your mess is foul, Kara. I never told Kory a lot of things I know about you. You act innocent, but I know better. I see you on social media quoting Bible verses. I saw you praying on Facebook one day. I was like, 'look at this shit'. You do not live the life you preach about. You go out of town every month. Bambi, Toni, Crush and Melanin go out of town at the same time. You all have been doing this since high school. Think back to our senior year. Football playoffs at Texas Stadium. After the game, me and some of the fellas went to a party over on Camp Wisdom Road. There was a stripper pole, and you danced your ass off. I still got the video, and Kory has never seen it. Maybe it's time for him to see it. Stop that fake ass crying. If my cousin dies, Texas won't be big enough for the both of us."

Kara stopped crying and turned red with anger. She put her hand in her purse and looked me in the eye.

"Let me tell you something, Mr. Big Baller wannabe. I sat up night after night waiting for Kory to come home. Most of the time he doesn't come home until the next day. If I say something to him, I get my butt kicked. He smells like liquor, drugs and nasty vagina. Seldom do we make love. He hardly works. The money he makes is spent on old cars and trucks. He also has a closet full of expensive clothes. He has more clothes than I do. There is a trunk in his closet full of jewelry or something. I don't know what's in it. Kory spends money on Kory. The only thing that he does care about is our daughters. I will give him that much."

"His daughters, Kara? Are they his daughters?"

Kara stood up and took her hand out of her purse. In her right hand is a black, Cobra two-shot Derringer. She moves close to me and straddles my left leg. Her left breast is pressed against my eye. The Derringer digs deep into my neck.

"Say it again, Wayne. Say Kory is not the father of my two girls. Go ahead, Big Baller. Say it."

I look at the people seated across from me. Everyone is moving in a hurry. Kara is crying, and her hand is on the trigger. Bambi walks over and whispers in Kara's ear. Kara removed the gun from my neck and put it back in her purse. She sat back down in her seat. I went to the bathroom.

When I returned from the bathroom, the nurse said the others went to Mr. Henderson's room. When I opened the door, I see them walking just ahead of me. I followed them to Kory's room. The doctor gave Kory a sedative. We all sat down. I watched Kara as she adjusted Kory's pillows. She tucked the covers in like you would a child's bed. Kara moved a chair close to Kory's bed and rubbed his head. She got a warm towel from his bathroom and cleaned his face. Then, she clipped his fingernails. Bambi sat quietly in a chair against the wall. She cried silently because she could see Kara really loved Kory. She dared not say anything. We all kept quiet. Kara got a gun.

I wonder why Kory seldom touched Kara. I remember Elvis Presley had a similar marriage. Elvis loved Pricilla, but he never touched her. He put Pricilla on a pedestal and admired her beauty. Pretty, little Pricilla was his queen.

We watched Kory sleep for a couple of hours. I took the girls home. Kara stayed the night with Kory.

* * * * *

Kara's Bleeding Heart

"Kory, I don't know if you can hear me, but I need to tell you something. There are some things that you don't know about me. I never told these things to anybody. When I was a little girl, my Daddy was a violent man. He was in and out of jail. He was violent toward my mother. My grandparents hated my father. They did not think he was good enough for my mother. My grandmother was white, and my grandfather was Mexican. My grandfather's family was well to do."

"They always told my mother she could do a lot better than my father. They said degrading things in the presence of my father. "Ghetto black man" was their favorite name for Daddy. My father grew angry because my mother never defended him to her parents. My father took his anger out on my mother. He developed a drinking problem and would leave home for weeks at a time. One time, Daddy left, and my grandparents came by our house. They moved our mother back to their house in Calexico, California. We didn't see her again until years later. When my dad returned home to see his four kids abandoned by their mother, he was furious.

Daddy hired a lady to take care of us while he was gone. Her name was Griselda. Griselda's friends, both men and women, came to visit her at our house. They were sexual partners. When she was lonely, she turned her sexual desires toward me and my siblings. Pandora's Box was opened, Kory.

My brother, Don, Jr., was the oldest at eleven years old. Griselda used to lock my brother in his bedroom closet. He could not get out because there was no knob on the other side of the door. My sister, Christina, was nine. I was eight, and my sister, Pinky, was six. We could not fight her off. One by one, she took us in her bedroom and locked the door.

She would not let us cry and hug each other. She kept our hair in pony tails. She used to braid one of Christina's pony tails to one of my pony tails. She braided my other pony tail to one of Pinky's pony tails. When we slept at night, she would tie Christina's other pony tail to the left side of the bed post. She then tied Pinky's other pony tail to the right side of the bedpost. She wrapped the ends of our hair with strings. The knot was too hard to untie. We did not understand why she treated us so bad. She was a crazy-ass bitch.

When Daddy returned home, we told him how she treated us. He didn't listen at first. But one day, Griselda came up missing. We never saw her again. Daddy never explained what happened to her.

During that same week, Daddy shot both of my grandparents. They didn't die, but Daddy went to prison. My siblings and I bounced around foster care for about nine months. Then, one day, our mom came to get us. We didn't understand why she left and why it took so long for her to come and get us. We are still trying to put pieces of our lives back together.

You see, my childhood is to blame for the way I am. I know right from wrong, but I cannot control myself. I keep in touch with my siblings, and they are all having relationship problems. We should all be in long-term therapy.

When you were a boy, I used to watch you when you were at your uncle's house. You and Wayne were the only two guys who still rode bicycles. Everyone else was playing video games. You were so cute and muscular. I remember the day I fell in love with you.

There was a trail between Cecil Avenue and Gentry Parkway that led to McDonald's. My siblings and I decided to go to McDonald's one day. On our way to McDonald's, some knucklehead guys tried to touch me. My brother tried to fight them off, but they overpowered him. You were riding in the trail coming from McDonald's. The knuckleheads were surprised when you jumped in and saved us. My hero was riding a ten-speed bicycle. You popped a wheelie and ran over both of those guys. That day was the highlight of my childhood. My sisters and my brother laughed out loud. We had a new friend.

I used to write your name on everything. Kory and Kara, Kara and Kory. All my notebooks had your name written on them. You were my escape from reality. When I went to middle school, you were the only boy that I enjoyed talking to. I was so excited to see you. My teddy bear's name was Kory. I never told you any of this before. You are unconscious, but I wanted you to know. Maybe one day things will get better. I have my own personal demons controlling my thoughts. Life is not supposed to be so dramatic.

I want to change, but I do not know how. Kory, please Kory, take our daughters and raise them. Marry a woman who can be a good mother to them. Keep them away from me. I don't want to ruin their lives. I am sorry for not being a good mother to them, Kory. I don't know what to do. Kory, are you waking up?"

"Kara, stop crying. I will do everything in my power to make sure our daughters grow up to be good women. But they will always know you as their mother. This Griselda woman ruined your life. It is not your fault. If I ever meet her, I will kill her. We both need fixing, Kara. We both need to change. Can't nobody fix us but the Lord. Let's pray, Kara, then I can sleep. I will always be here for you, Kara, I promise."

"Thank you for not getting mad, Kory. I love you, Kory. Go to sleep. I will stay here with you."

* * * * *

Kara Apologizes

"Wake up Kory. The nurse is here to take your vital signs."

"Kory, I am Nurse Beverly. How are you feeling this morning?"

Rolling over from his side to his back,

"I feel pretty good, Nurse Beverly."

"The doctor will be in around 7:00 am with further instructions."

Kory replied,

"Thank you, nurse Beverly."

Nurse Beverly completes her work.

"See you later, Mr. Kory."

Kory smiles at Nurse Beverly as she exits.

While the door is open, Wayne enters.

"Kinfolk, how you doing?"

"Wayne, what's up? I am feeling a lot better, cuz. I did not expect to see you this early in the morning. Kara stayed the night with me."

Wayne looked at me and spoke.

"Hey, Kara."

"Hi, Wayne."

I leaned over and kissed Kory goodbye.

"Kory, I have to go check on the girls. I will be back later today. Wayne walk out with me, please?"

Wayne had an unsure look on his face.

"Ok, Kara."

The two of us walked outside of the doorway. I faced Wayne and looked him in the eye.

"Wayne, I am sorry about last night."

He had a look on his face like he thought I was going to shoot him. He stuttered when talking.

"Kara, you do not have to apologize. I understand. There are some things a man should never say to a woman. Especially when it comes to her kids. The line will not be crossed again."

I smiled,

"Wayne, I know you and Kory are just like brothers. Watch Kory's back and keep him safe for me, please?"

Looking at Wayne, I cried.

"Stop crying, Kara. I got Kory's back. Go home and take care of the kids."

We hugged, and I went home to my kids. Wayne went back into Kory's room.

* * * * *

White Cadillac

"Kory, I have been riding around all night long."

Looking at Wayne, I agreed with him.

"You look sleepy, Wayne. Pull up a chair."

"I did some checking around last night, Kory. I think I know who shot at us. Somebody told me where he will be later today. Today might be his last day on earth."

I looked at Wayne and shook my head.

"No, Wayne. We need a plan. We need to put a lot of thought into a good plan. Today is not the day. Wait until I have healed. We will take his ass out."

"Well, let me tell you what happened last night, Kory. Me and the girls drove around Loop 323. We stopped at the red light in front of Sam's Club. A white, old-school Cadillac pulled up on the right side of my car. The girls suddenly looked away from the car and put their hands on the side of their face. I was like, 'what the hell is going on?' The guy in the Cadillac must be an undercover cop or something. But nooo, I remembered. There was a show on PAY TV years ago, that explained the reaction from the girls. The show was "Pimps Up, Ho's Down." Do you remember, Kory?"

I put my hand on my head and looked at Wayne in disbelief.

"Wayne, I recorded that show. It's in my collection. When the doctor releases me, we are going to my house and check it out."

Wayne interrupted me.

"Hold up, Kory. Check this out. We get to the Cascades Apartments, and I confronted the girls. I parked the car and we talked. 'Toni, Melanin, Crush and Bambi. Tell me how I missed this? We have known each other since high school. Why did I not know about your extracurricular activities? They got quiet. Damn it, I know you all hear me'."

Bambi turned and looked me in the eye.

"You were not supposed to know, Wayne. When we are with you, we have a good time. We are friends. We are classmates, and we care about you. It is not business with you. You make us laugh, and you protect us. We feel safe with you."

I turned where I could see all the girls at the same time.

"I feel stupid. You all could have let me in on your secret."

Toni, sitting in the back seat, leaned forward and touched my shoulder.

"Then what, Wayne? You would have looked at us in a different way."

Melanin and Crush leaned forward and touched my hand.

"Wayne, don't be mad. We need an escape away from the bullshit. You are the realest person we know. You and your cousin, Kory, are nice guys."

Bambi laughed.

"Do not get mad, Wayne. You and your cousin, Kory, want to be Big Ballers. The two of you are not Big Ballers. The world does not need another Big Baller. It is good to know there are still some good black men left."

The girls all agreed. Bambi touched my face.

"Wayne when I stop living this bullshit life, I want a good man. Right now, I do what I want to do. We like to party, make money and live the high life. We are free to do whatever we want to do."

I looked at the girls and shook my head.

"If you all are free to do what you want to do, why did you turn your head at the red light? Tell the truth. There are gaps in your story."

They laughed. Bambi continued.

"Let it go, Wayne. Please just be our friend like you have always been. And stop looking sad, Wayne. We love you."

Toni and Melanin both agreed.

"Yeah, Wayne, we love you. Do not stop loving us."

Crush ran in the house like she was sick. I looked at the girls.

"I will keep loving you all, but do not lie to me again."

Getting out of the car, Toni looked back at me.

"We did not lie, Wayne."

I pointed my finger at all of them.

"Not telling all of the information is the same as lying. Good night. Leave it like that."

The girls responded as they walked to their apartment.

"Good night, Wayne."

Toni walked behind the other girls.

"Toni, come here."

I opened the driver's side door and scooted the seat back.

"Give me a hug, Toni."

"What are you doing, Wayne? I knew you wanted me. What took you so long?"

I sat Toni in my lap.

"Toni, tonight made me think about what is real in life. I don't want to die without loving someone. I also want to be loved in return. Plus, I want some kids. I listen to stripper's conversation when I'm in the club. They all say the same thing. I will dance for a few years, so I can make some money. Then I will stop and get married. The thing is, they can't stop. The money gets good and they die as old, worn out strippers. They never fall in love. Speaking for myself, I don't want nothing worn out. I won't wait on you forever. You got a surprised look on your face, Toni."

Toni looked at me with eyes wide open and forehead stretched upward.

"Wayne, I can stop. I just like hanging with the girls. If you really want to love me, I will stop. But you need to stop your bullshit, too."

I smiled and hugged Toni.

"Consider it done, Toni. I'm in."

* * * * *

Kory leaves the Hospital

The doctor released me from the hospital on Saturday morning. Wayne picked me up.

"Man, I am glad to be going home. The doctor hesitated about releasing me. They want me to follow up with my primary care physician in three weeks. I need to chill so I can go to work Monday. After I am one hundred percent, I will find the son of a bitch that shot at us. But before we find him, we need to go in the woods. We need to practice shooting, Wayne."

Walking through the back gate, I noticed the grill was still smoking.

"Wayne, open the door on the grill."

"Ok, Kory. This bad boy is still warm. Hey, man, there is something wrapped in foil."

Both of us look at the brisket wrapped in foil and laughed. Wayne looked over at me and spoke.

"We are about to eat the hell out of this brisket."

I opened the back door and got a foil pan from the cabinet.

"Wayne, do me a favor and put the brisket in this pan. The foil is full of juice. That is a black angus brisket. They are tender and juicy. Bring it in the house and put it on the island. Let me put a couple of potatoes in the microwave. I will get some buttered, split-top bread from the bread box. I don't have but a little barbeque sauce left Wayne. No worry, I'll just add some water and pancake syrup to it."

"Kory, what did you say?"

"I know that sounds funny, Wayne. But I've been doing it for years. Once I warm up the sauce in the microwave it will taste so good. You will slap your mama and tell her to wake up. She must be dreaming. It's not supposed to taste this good."

"In a few minutes, we will have a meal fit for two Big Ballers."

We both laughed.

"Have a seat at the table, Wayne. Let me slice off some of the juicy, tender brisket. This bad boy is good."

With juice dripping from his goatee, Wayne smiled and shook his head yes.

"Yeah, you right, Kory, but first I want to see that video. I need more information to help me figure some things out."

"Ok, Wayne. Let's move to the family room. There should be some TV trays already set up."

I put the VHS tape in, and Wayne was on the edge of his seat.

"Pimps UP Ho's Down. Yeah, that's the right one, Kory. Fast forward until you get to the part about a prostitute looking a pimp in the eye. Ok, stop right there. Let's see what this guy is talking about. Let it play from that point."

That is a real pimp right there, Kory. Listen to him talk.

"The game of pimping is an art. Everyone cannot pimp. Your working girls have got to know their place. In the presence of a pimp, a working girl is required to hold her head down. She is not allowed to call a pimp by his name. The pimp takes all the money. A working girl is also required to tattoo a pimp's name on her thigh. If she looks another pimp in his eye, she is said to have reckless eye problems. If she violates the rules, a pimp can put her on pimp arrest. Pimp arrest means she must give up all her jewelry, money or anything of value."

"That's it, Kory. Now I understand. The guy in the white Cadillac was a pimp. When he pulled up next to me at the red light, Bambi, Melanin, Crush and Toni turned and looked the other way. Damn, that's messed up."

Wayne sat back on the couch staring in disbelief. I looked at him and shook my head.

"If they are prostitutes, who is their pimp?"

Wayne shook his head and looked at me.

"Kory, that's the same thing I am trying to figure out. Let's ride, Kory."

With car keys in hand, Wayne hurried toward the front door.

"Kory, you coming?"

Slowly getting up from my recliner, I answered.

"Wayne, I need to chill, man."

Wayne slowly walked back through the house to where I was sitting.

"Kory, you just got out of the hospital. You can't go. I forgot, cuz. My bad. Get some rest, and I will check with you tomorrow."

Slowly falling to sleep, I answered.

"Sounds good, Wayne. You should go home and chill yourself."

"We need time to get a plan together. We also need to shoot the guns some more. Tonight is not the night. We do not have enough information yet. Once we get enough information, we need to wait for a cold wintry night to execute our plan."

Wayne has a confused look on his face.

"Kory, why do we need to wait for a cold, wintry night? We need to take care of business as quickly as possible."

I turned the television down and explained.

"It's like this, Wayne. We can't just roll up on somebody with guns blazing and shoot innocent people. We must get close enough to the shooter to make sure we don't miss. If we miss, we die. It is easy to hide a gun inside of an overcoat. Go home, Wayne."

Wayne had a little half grin on his face.

"You know, Kory, you are a lot smarter these days. I'll be in touch."

"Ok, Wayne, be easy."

* * * * *

Wayne Investigates

"Hello."

The voice on the other end of the phone responds.

"Hello, is this Kory?

"Yeah, this is Kory. Who is this calling me at 3:45 on Sunday morning?

"Kory, this is Slim Janky. I met you at The Gambling Shack the night a crazy woman cut you with a knife."

"Yeah, yeah, Slim Janky. I remember you. Thanks for helping me, man. What's going on?"

"Kory, your cousin, Wayne, told me to call you. He is in Mother's Hospital. He is in the emergency room."

I took a deep breath before responding.

"Slim Janky, what happened to Wayne?"

"Man, I will tell you when I see you."

"Ok, let me get dressed, and I will be there in a minute. Thanks for calling."

"Ok, Kory, I will see you when you get here."

Humm, I wonder if I should take my gun. Yeah, I better take my Smith and Wesson. There might be trouble. I put my gun underneath the seat of my truck and hurried to the hospital. I parked and went to the emergency room. Breaking in line, I spoke to the nurse at the desk.

"Nurse, I am here to see Wayne Henderson. He was brought here earlier tonight."

The nurse checked the computer and directed me to Wayne's room.

I found Wayne, and Slim Janky was with him. Wayne is unconscious.

"What the hell happened?"

"Kory, what's up, man? Wayne was jumped by some guys at The Party Shack. I am not exactly sure what happened because I was outside. Wayne told me to stay outside. He said if I need you, come in blasting. So, I stayed outside talking to some women."

"Slim, Wayne left my house headed home. Where did the two of you meet?"

Slim Janky shook his head and began to explain.

"Let's walk out in the hallway, Kory."

The two of us walk out into the hallway.

"This is what happened, Kory. I was up on Morris Street at the pool hall. A lot of things happen at the pool hall. Drugs, gambling, bootlegging, fighting, prostitution, snitching--you name it. It happens on Morris Street. We were all standing outside drinking and smoking. It was business as usual. We do what we do and watch for Tyler police. Wayne asked if somebody had been on Morris Street acting a fool. As you know, somebody acts a fool on Morris Street every day. So, we all laughed at him. The younger guys who didn't know Wayne thought he was a snitch. The two of us decided to go inside the pool hall to get a beer."

"As soon as we stepped inside the building, somebody did a drive by shooting. People were scrambling, trying to get out of the way. Everyone, except Wayne. After the car passed, it stopped at the corner of Palace Street. Wayne ran into the street trying to see who was doing the shooting. After he saw the car, he ran back inside the pool hall. People were still hiding."

Wayne said,

"It's a white Cadillac. Who drives an old-school white Cadillac? Does anybody know?"

"Now people are starting to talk. Somebody finally said, that's Big Tilley. He's from Louisiana. He is trying to take over. If you are making money doing anything, he wants in. Drugs, liquor, gambling, prostitution, it doesn't matter. The word on the street is he killed somebody in Longview. A ruthless killer is trying to take over the crime world in Tyler, Texas. How about that for small-town crime?"

* * * * *

The PoPo

"Wayne ran to his car, and I followed him. My stupid ass got in the car with Wayne. Big Tilley was driving slow like he did not have a worry in the world. He was really gangster. I told Wayne not to follow this guy too close. Then, the police stopped us."

Seeing the cop walk from his car to our car made us nervous. Wayne rolled the window down.

"What up, popo?"

I interrupted,

"How are you doing, officer?"

He responded,

"I need to see your license and registration please? Do you know why I stopped you?"

Wayne responded.

"No, officer, I don't. Why did you stop me?"

The officer responded.

"I stopped you for suspicious behavior. You were driving 35 in a 45. Also, you have three windows up and one window down. In my years of being a police officer, that's a sign of drug usage."

Wayne told him.

"Officer, the windows on the car go up and down."

I interrupted Wayne before he got us arrested.

"Officer I can explain why that window is down."

The officer walked around to the passenger side where I was. He began his interrogation of me.

"Explain why the window is down."

So, I explained.

"Officer, we got lactose."

He looked at me like I was crazy. He repeated what I said.

"You got lactose?"

I responded,

"Yes, sir, officer. You see, officer, we went to my grandmama's house for lunch. We spent most of the day at my grandmama's house. She cooked one heck of a meal and after dinner she made some homemade ice cream. You know the kind that is hand churned with extra vanilla flavoring. She doesn't have the electric ice cream maker. She has the old style. You got to turn it with your hand. I bet that is why my arm is sore. Anyway, you pack that dry ice around the cylinder and turn until you make ice cream. Hell, we ate it all. It's the best ice cream you ever had. And that's how we ended up with lactose."

The officer replied,

"You mean you are lactose intolerant, don't you?"

"Yeah, that's what I said."

"The police started laughing. He was still asking us questions."

"You mean to tell me that both of you are lactose intolerant at the same time?"

I replied,

"That's right, officer. My stomach is bubbling gas right now. I might need to let the other three windows down."

"The police officer was still laughing."

He responded.

"You know, I needed a good laugh. And that is the most original excuse I have ever heard. I'll be back in a minute."

He walked back to his car and slumped over the hood. I looked back and saw he was having a good laugh. He waved us on and we took off. Finally, the officer let us go. We continued driving in the same direction. The white Cadillac was nowhere in sight.

"We were close to The Gambling Shack, so we turned into the parking lot. There sat the white Cadillac. Wayne was like; 'let's go bust a cap in his big butt'. But we didn't have a gun. Wayne had a plan. He said he was going inside to check out things. He wanted me to stay outside, and he would call me if he needed help. I told Wayne it was a bad idea, but he wanted to see who was driving the white Cadillac."

"Kory, are y'all talking about me? I'm not sleep. Come closer."

Me and Slim walked from the doorway and took a seat next to Wayne's bed. I asked Wayne,

"How you feeling, cuz?"

With only one eye open, he turned his head toward me.

"My head hurt. That fat sombitch knocked the hell out of me. My head is ringing. He should have killed me. I promise I will see him again. Kory, you hear me?"

I adjusted Wayne's pillow.

"I hear you, Wayne. But this one is on me. I got this Wayne."

Wayne grabbed my forearm.

"Kory, wait for me. You cannot do it by yourself. There are three of them. Three blood brothers. They are all violent. Do not try it by yourself. Give me a chance to heal, kinfolk. Sit down, Kory. I know you are mad, dawg. Let me tell you what happened."

"I walked in The Party Shack and took a seat at the bar. I ordered a shot of Crown Royal and a Modelo beer."

The bartender asked,

"Do we have Modelo, Tilley?" The big guy answered,

"Yeah. Look in the green and white cooler."

So that's Big Tilley, I thought to myself.

"I sat there for a while and listened to the conversation across the room at the crap table. They were talking about how they took the bar from the owner, Skippy

Jack. I noticed none of the regular people were there. The woman in the miniskirt was not there either. The bar stool where she normally sat was occupied by Big Tilley."

"The three brothers, Alonzo, Sly, and Big Tilly are running the crap table. Alonzo and Sly are standing on opposite ends of the table. Big Tilley is the houseman. He stands with his back against the wall. The table is pushed up close to the wall next to the staircase."

"I walked up to the table and took a position. The houseman said it's a twenty dollar buy in and ten dollars a game. I said *cool* and give him the money. The guy next to me rolled a four on the come-out roll. Before the dice stopped rolling, Alonzo and Sly started taking money from everyone. I told Sly to get his damn hands off my money. He copped an attitude, and we almost had a fight."

"Finally, it was my turn to roll. I held my money in my hand while I rolled. Big Tilley looked at me like he wanted to bite my head off. I rolled a three. I rolled again and made my point. I got paid good money. Now, all three brothers are standing with arms folded. They look like three lions staring at a buffalo. I'm the buffalo. Big Tilley tells me, 'Play, got damn it.' He has the voice of a big gut, Baptist preacher. I laughed at him, and he became even madder. Then, I told him his big poke-chop ass need to wipe the grease off his chin. *You a nasty Cadillac driving punk.* I probably shouldn't have said that."

"Alonzo was standing to my left. He took a swing at me, and I dodged it. I hit him right on the chin, and he dropped. Before I could recover, Big Tilley hit me over the head with something. That's all I remember. The doctor said I have a concussion."

"Somebody is knocking at the door. Come in. Oh, come on in Nurse Christina."

"I need to check your vitals, Mr. Henderson. How are you feeling?"

"Nurse, my head is hurting."

"I have some pain medicine for you, Mr. Henderson. I will put it in your IV before I leave. You are running a slight temperature. Your blood pressure is high as well. You will have to get plenty of rest to heal properly. This shot will knock you out."

"Thank you, Nurse Christina. Close the door behind you, please."

"Ok, Mr. Henderson. If you need anything, press the button on the remote."

"Kory, they got another nurse that comes in my room at random. I don't even think he works on this floor. He just shows up unannounced. He comes in here fanning the sheets talking about he's checking my bed pan. I'm not on a bed pan. Dang, my head is hurting. Why are y'all laughing?"

"Somebody is coming in, Wayne."

"Mr. Henderson, how are you doing?"

Wayne answered,

"Kory, that's the sombitch right there. I'm not on no got damn bed pan. You are just roaming the hall talking to random men. Get your ass out of here. Ain't nothing funny. Kory, why are you and Slim Janky laughing? Throw his butt out. My head is hurting."

The nurse replied,

"I am a good nurse, Mr. Henderson. I am just doing my job. Good night, sir."

"Kory, don't you leave until that 7'2" nurse leaves. Let me have your gun, Kory. I guarantee he will be back. When he comes back, I will shoot his tall butt."

We all laughed.

"Wayne, calm down and go to sleep. I will see you tomorrow. Slim Janky, let's go. I need to call my job and tell them I am sick."

* * * * *

Kory Scopes out The Party Shack

"Kory, if you don't mind, drop me off at my sister's house.   She lives in the housing addition behind 12 Oaks Motel."

"Ok, will do Slim Janky."

The Gambling Shack was about fifteen minutes away from his sister's house. I dropped Slim Janky off and stopped by The Gambling Shack for a moment.

The sun is coming up and everyone is gone for the night.   There are a few people moving around in the parking lot.   The last time I was here, there was an attempt on my life in this parking lot. Looks like they changed the name from Gambling Shack to Party Shack. I wonder what the place looks like inside.

I drove up close to the guy picking up beer cans in the parking lot.

"Hey man. What's going on?"

He replied,

"Everyone is gone man. We are cleaning up."

I replied,

"Is anybody inside?"

He tied a wire tie on the trash bag and answered.

"Yeah."

"Do you think they would mind if I looked inside? I have never been inside this place."

He shook his head no.

"Go ahead and look. There is not much to look at. It's a hay barn."

I parked my truck and got out. It is cool outside. The temperature has really dropped the last couple of days. Texas weather is unpredictable. One day it feels like spring, and the next day the temperature is freezing.

A strange looking woman met me at the front door. She asked,

"Are you looking for something, sexy?"

I replied,

"I have never seen the inside of this building. Just curious to see what it looks like."

She put one arm around my waste and hugged me from the side. She used her other hand to massage my chest.

"Go upstairs and wait for me. I am the best around. It will not take me long, I promise. I will give you the time of your life."

I answered,

"Ok."

I hate smelling liquor and cigarettes on a woman's breath. Walking fast, I looked at the place as best I could. I tried my best to avoid the liquor-breath female. This strange looking female saw me walking toward the front door and tried to stop me.

"Hey, where are you going? Slow down. I thought you were going to wait for me."

Her voice got louder as I walked out of the front door.

"Come back next weekend. The Old-School Cruisers are having a car show next Saturday. Everyone will be here. Come and enjoy yourself. Bye, sexy."

I rushed back to my truck and sped away before the woman could catch up with me.

Tuesday morning, I picked up Wayne from the hospital. The two of us rested up for a week or so. This is the first time I listened to a doctor's instructions. I thought I was dying. I also thought my cousin was dying.

We are both blessed to be alive.

* * * * *

Pinging Bullets

I need to get ready for the inevitable, so I get out of bed focused. I need to make sure my weapons are still in good working condition. Some of them may need oiling. After checking my guns, I walk into the woods behind my house. Here we go. *Pow, pow, pow, pow, pow. Tat-tat-tat, tat-tat-tat, tat-tat-tat, tat-tat-tat.* A voice is shouting.

"Hey! Who is that shooting behind my house?"

I answer,

"Mordell, it's Kory. I'm getting some target practice in. Where are you?"

"I'm behind the big oak tree to your right. Your bullets are ricocheting off the trees. Hold your fire, Kory. I'm walking down the hill where you are."

The two of us shake hands.

"What's up, Mordell? How are you doing?"

Mordell laughed and held his side.

"Hell, I was doing pretty good until I heard the *ping, ping, ping* bouncing off the trees. What the hell, Kory? You haven't shot a gun in a long time. You need a lot of practice. A bullet hit my dog house. You scared my dog, Kory!"

Slightly embarrassed, I responded.

"Man, I am so sorry. And you're right. It's been a while since the last time I shot a gun."

Mordell laughed even harder.

"Yeah, I can tell. Why did you wait for it to turn cold to shoot Kory?"

I didn't want to make an excuse. So, I shrugged my shoulders.

"No reason, man."

Mordell is still laughing and talking.

"Erik is on the way down the hill."

Mordell and I both look up at the top of the hill. Mordell continues.

"You know, Erik is an ex-Marine."

I give Mordell a firm go to hell look.

"Well Mr. Mordell, I was in the Army myself. It's just been a while that's all."

Mordell looked back at me and laughed.

173

"What did you do in the Army, Kory?"

I answered him with pride.

"After basic training, I worked in supply. That was my job. You don't need a gun in the supply room."

Mordell stopped laughing for a minute.

"O…k, Kory. I had forgotten. There's Erik. He can teach us both how to shoot. Erik, Kory is the shooter."

Erik walks down the hill. Erik and Mordell lean on each other's shoulders and laugh. Erik repeated what Mordell said.

"Kory is the shooter? That is funny. I brought my AK47. I thought we were being attacked, Kory."

The two of them carried on for a while about my shooting. Finally, I spoke up for myself.

"Erik, that is not funny. I have an AK47 of my own, thank you. It has a bump stock on it; although, it has been a while since I shot it. I thought it might be a good idea for me to start with this Smith & Wesson MP shield 40. After I feel comfortable with this gun, then I will get the automatic stuff."

Both Erik and Mordell look at me with question.

"Automatic? What automatic, Kory?"

They stop laughing.

"Well fellas, let's just say, I got some toys in my chest. The two of you will be surprised what I have."

Erik looks at Mordell.

"Mordell, Kory is lying. And if he is not lying, let's go get the toy chest."

Mordell agreed,

"Yeah, Kory. I agree with Erik. Let's go get the toy chest."

"Ok, fellas. Let's walk back up the hill to my house. You guys are in for a shocking surprise."

"Erik, have a seat around the pool while me and Mordell bring out the toy chest."

Mordell and I grab the chest and bring it outside. We sat the chest in front of Erik. I open and watch the expressions on their faces. Erik hesitates then speaks.

"Oh ... my ... goodness. Kory, I stand corrected. Mordell, Kory is a hitman."

Mordell is going through the chest like a kid opening presents on Christmas day.

"Kory, I don't even know the names of most of these weapons."

I named the weapons in my chest to my friends as best I could.

"Let's see I got a Seburo CX, a Luger 60, a Gilboa automatic pistol, Uzi submachine gun that folds in half. Let's see, what else? Oh yeah, a Baikal MP-461 Strazhnik, a MAT-49 submachine gun, and check out this AF2011-A1 Double Barrel Pistol. This bad boy is nice. Also, this is a 454-magnum revolver with a 30mm grenade launcher. The rest of these guns--I don't know what they are. So, what do you guys think? What do you think Erik, Mr. Marine?"

Erik has a look of satisfaction on his face.

"Kory, I stand in amazement. You are definitely the man."

"Kory, where did you get all these nice weapons? These bad boys are fully automatic."

"Erik, if I tell you I got to kill you."

Everyone laughed.

"Kory, go ahead and kill me. I have got to talk to your source."

So, I leaned in real close.

"Ok fellas. It's like this. I was in Chicago with an associate."

Erik was too curious.

"Kory, who do you know in Chicago?"

Looking at Mordell.

"Man, I know people. Anyway, this associate of mine and I were in Chicago. We were hanging out in the wee hours of the morning. My associate tells me to scoot down in the seat. I looked at him like, 'What's going on?' He then turns into a dark alley. Keep in mind, we are in the hood. We get about halfway through the alley and he stops the car. Now, I'm tripping because I don't have a gun. He gets out of the car and gets a crow bar from his trunk. There are about four crates spread out next to each other. They were placed just out of the path of the car. He opened one of the crates and there were guns like I have never seen. This was military equipment. The pistols were fully automatic. In fact, everything in the crate was automatic. There was ammo for all the guns and extra magazines. We loaded two crates into the trunk of his old-school car and burned rubber leaving. Fellas, I was so nervous. Anyway, to make a long story short, I rented a van to get the weapons back to Texas. Check my Facebook page to verify my story. I shared a link that my associate posted!"

Erik could not resist.

"Kory, first, these weapons are illegal. They are Israeli, German and Russian. Not to mention being fully automatic. Don't get caught with these weapons, Kory. You said they were in an alley?"

"Yeah, Erik, in Chicago."

Erik looked at Mordell.

"Mordell, what do you think?"

Mordell looked at Kory.

"Kory, I think it is fair to say that the war in Chicago is real. It is also being funded by some high rank person in the government. Gang members don't have access to military weapons. Somebody wants us to kill each other. Seeing these weapons breaks my heart. If this is true, the war in Chicago will not end until we are all dead."

A sad look came over Mordell's face. I responded,

"I feel you, Mordell. I won't be going back to Chicago any time soon."

I notice Mordell staring into space.

"Mordell, why are you staring at me? I see your little brain working. What's up?"

Mordell laughed,

"Well, you read me pretty good, Kory. My question is when are we going to do this? When is the big pay back going down?"

I looked at Mordell and Erik. Then looked up at the sky.

"Fellas, the weather is working in our favor. We can hide our guns inside our overcoats and not be noticed. They are having a car show at The Party Shack Saturday. The big payback is going down this weekend."

* * * * *

The Big Payback

The rest of the week I thought about what was about to happen this weekend. I don't want to die. But I refuse to look over my shoulder for the rest of my life.

I arrived at The Party Shack as the sun was going down. The parking lot was full. People are everywhere. As I parked my car, my phone rang.

"Kory, where are you? Hey man, we been waiting on you to call. We're sitting in your driveway. Kory, it's Wayne. Mordell and Erik are here, too."

Reluctant to answer,

"Fellas, I'm at The Party Shack."

Wayne screamed.

"Why the hell are you there by yourself? You know we got your back, man!"

I stood next to my truck and talked.

"Wayne, you should be in bed."

The fellas were talking in the background.

"Run the stop sign! Hurry up!"

"Wayne, Erik, Mordell, I couldn't wait. This is something I have to do by myself. I owe it to Kara."

"Kory, you don't owe her nothing. She's not the woman you think she is. There is a lot you don't know about Kara."

"Wayne, it doesn't matter. My future depends on tonight. I'm not going out like a punk. I'm walking up to Big Tilley and butting heads with him, WWE. Then I will fill his butt with bullet holes, reload and do it again."

With tears running down my face, I continued.

"Fellas, if I don't make it, I had a good time doing it."

Wayne won't stop shouting.

"Hurry up and get there, Mordell. They will kill my cousin. Kory, got damn it! We are on the way. Put your headset on so we can all talk to each other--the headset we use when we play paintball."

I walked around to the passenger side of the truck and opened the door. The headset was in the glove box. I put it on.

"Ok, Wayne, I just put on my headset. I'm going in. May the Lord be with me."

Wayne kept screaming.

"Kory! Kory! Kory! got dang it!"

I put on my hat, leaned it to the side and turned up the collar on my coat. Hoping not to be recognized, I walked slowly across the field. I hear Wayne and the fellas talking loud in my headset. They are driving hard and fast, breaking every law. They will be here soon, but I can't wait.

Everyone who can pay is welcomed inside. There is no security search. I walked through the door and blended in with the crowd. There are so many people here. It's kind of like being in Home Depot on Black Friday. Tables are spaced strategically, and people are dancing in between them. I have never seen so many women kissing and fondling each other. *Get a man.*

The Party Shack is a hay barn with a loft and tall ceilings. Bales of hay are stacked sporadically throughout the barn. People are dancing and drinking on both levels. The crap table is a little less than a hundred and fifty feet inside the door to the left. The stairway has a platform half way up.

I maneuver my way to the official dance floor, which is located three fourths of the way into the building. Crossing the dance floor, the crap table is in my view.

In a few minutes, I will be butting heads with Big Tilley.

"Kory, can you hear me?"

"Yeah, Wayne, I hear you."

"Kory, that's him. I hear Big Tilley."

"Wayne, there are a lot of people talking. I see three people behind the crap table. Which one is Big Tilley?"

"Kory, Big Tilley is the one with the hat on that looks like a preacher. He has a deep voice and a slight stutter. He talks slow, and it doesn't take much to piss him off. He has a short fuse. He likes to order people around."

"I'm too far away from the table to hear their voices, Wayne. Plus, the music is kind of loud. I will have to get closer."

"Damn it! I wanted to be nose to nose with this guy, Wayne. Looks like I will have to execute him from a distance."

I am getting pissed off. My overcoat has every possible weapon I could bring with me with extra magazines to match. Sweat is running down my back as my hand grips the trigger tighter.

"There are people standing behind the players at the crap table ten deep. The place is full of women. Breaking in line will only bring unwanted attention to myself. There may only be one chance for a clear shot."

"Kory, we are here. Mordell is in the front parking lot. Erik is coming inside. I'm going around to the back. Everyone who comes out is getting shot. Walk up the stairway and hang over the rail, Kory. That will put you up close with the crap table. You will have a clear shot without shooting innocent people."

"Ok Wayne, I'm headed to the stairway now."

"Excuse me. Excuse me. Can I get by you, please? Thank you. Let me step in between the two of you. You got some pretty legs. Ok, I made it to the stairway platform, Wayne."

There are three guys standing behind the crap table. All three of them are dressed alike. They are wearing black hats with matching arm bands over their biceps. A white bow tie is worn with a ruffled, tuxedo shirt. The three of them are dancing and tossing dice back and forth to each other. One of the guys is flirting with a female at the front of the table. People are standing around her and I am unable to see her body or her face. He keeps calling her, Miss Ma'am.

184

Standing on the platform of this stairway, my hands sweat as my anger increases. I take one last look at the crowd as my body goes numb. A set of eyes focused on me. Melanin is standing in a group of women about ten feet from the crap table. She spotted me right away. She's shaking her head no. It's too late. Tonight, I will die or evolve into greatness.

I take the stairs upward to the loft. Walking to the middle of the loft, I position myself against the hand rail. I am directly in front of the crap table. Looking downward, I lift my foot and place it on the middle rail. My cigar is wet, and half chewed.

"Sir, would you like a drink?"

Not making any sudden moves, I relax and order a drink. I cannot get a clear shot. There is a huge ceiling fan hanging from a joist that runs from wall to wall. I feel the wind as the blade turns. A huge, flat screen TV is hanging from the ceiling joist on the opposite side of the room. The volume turned up while the band takes a break.

A loud, deep, intimidating voice echoes through the shack.

"Play, got damn it."

My cousin is screaming in the headset that I am wearing.

"Kory, that's him! That's Big Tilley!! Shoot him! Shoot his big butt!"

"Copy that, Wayne. I got this."

The movie playing on the TV is "Tombstone." Doc Holiday is speaking.

"Why Johnny Ringo, you look like somebody just walked over your grave."

I walk back down to the stairway platform. With my guns set on full burst, I open fire at the guys behind the crap table. May God have mercy on my soul.

Tat-tat-tat, pow, pow, bang, bang, tat-tat-tat, tat-tat-tat, boom, boom, pow, pow, tat-tat-tat, tat-tat-tat, tat-tat-tat, boom, boom, bang, bang.

People are running and screaming. A petite woman is hiding in the crowd peeping around the others at me. The people in front of the crap table are falling and hiding on the floor. Now, the woman is standing all alone. She looks in my eyes as she points her gun at me. We both stop shooting and lower our weapons. I don't believe it. The woman is Kara... my wife. We were surprised to see each other. Then, she smiled at me. I motion for her to get down. She follows my instructions without question.

The lights go out as my cousin and best friends come through the front door with guns blazing. A lot of guns are in this shack. All I can see is red sparks flying in the air. I jump off the platform onto the bales of hay stacked next to the stairs. The shooting stopped. I walk toward the crap table with my guns ready to shoot. A single shot fires, *pow*. Kara stands up with the smoking gun. She jumps in my arms and wraps her legs around my waist. We hug, and she gives me a kiss that would shame the devil. No questions asked. No conversation needed. With caution, we walk out of the front door of The Party Shack. I hold Kara close under my right arm. We slowly released until our fingers touch. Walking in opposite directions we say our goodbyes. We all leave in separate vehicles. Sometime soon we will talk about tonight's event. Until then, new beginnings are inevitable.

* * * * *

Aftermath

Weeks later the events of that night weigh heavy on my mind. I feel like I'm being watched.

"Hello," the voice answered.

"Kory, what going on, man?"

"Wayne, what's up, man? I was sitting at home bouncing my head off the wall. But now I'm on the way to the car wash."

"Kory, man you said a mouthful. I am losing my mind, too. We still need to lay low and let things cool off. But realistically I don't think there will be much of an investigation. Big Tilley and his brothers were big time criminals. Law enforcement will probably give us a reward for solving a string of unsolved murders."

I hesitated before speaking to Wayne.

"I tell you what, Wayne, you go ahead and collect those rewards and put the money on your books in prison. As a matter of fact, you can have my share of the reward. I have another plan, Wayne."

"What's the plan, Kory?"

"For me it's important that I make some profound changes in my life. A new direction is inevitable. My wife and daughters need a good man. I need to change not only for them, but I need to change for me. Going to jail or to the graveyard should not be an alternative for me. There is only one way that I can think of to fix my life and everything around me. So, early Sunday morning I will be in service. Why don't you meet me there, Wayne?"

I can hear Wayne laughing.

"You know what, Kory? My mom and dad have been telling me the same thing. Maybe, I will see you there. Got to hang up, Kory. I'm spending time with Toni today. She wants to go shopping so we can dress alike. The two of us are a lot closer since that night at The Party Shack. When you are looking death in the face, it puts things in perspective. I think I'm beginning to realize what's important in life. Anyway, I'll see you later Kory."

"Ok, Wayne. See you later."

* * * * *

Church

The church parking lot is full. Maybe I will just go back home. Instead of parking on the church parking lot, I'll park on the street. What if somebody recognizes me from The Party Shack? I should have dyed my hair or shaved it all off. My heart is beating fast, and my underarms are sweating. God, please don't let me pass out. I wonder where the bathroom is. My stomach is not feeling so good. Keep your mouth shut and don't talk to anyone. No excuses. I am going inside.

Upon entering the church, the usher gave me a visitor's card. When I was a little boy, I ran around this church playing with my friends. Taking the card, I told her that I grew up in this church. But it's apparent that I haven't been here in a long time. She laughed and said,

"Welcome home," while giving me several tithe envelopes.

I told her, "I don't need but one envelope."

Holding her head downward and looking over her glasses she replied, "You might want to play catch up. The church needs the money."

We both laughed, and I put the extra envelopes in my suit coat pocket. She is so pretty. Maybe I should join the usher board. She set my mind at ease. I'm feeling a little better now.

Sermon

Pastor Taylor begins his sermon.

"This morning's sermon comes from the gospel of … Wait a minute. I look around the congregation and it seems that a lot of you are using iPhones and iPads. Some of you are on social media. The rest of you may be playing games. Let's do this. Everyone google sermon forgiving yourself. Scroll down to the second point, Forgiving Yourself. Now let's talk."

"This information is based on 2 Corinthians 5:17, Therefore if any man be in Christ, he is a new creature: old things are passed away; behold, all things are become new. This means that if you look at yourself in the mirror and you don't like what you see, forgive yourself. Learn how to be the person that God made you to be."

Somehow, Pastor Taylor got my information and is directing his sermon toward me. He's looking at me, and my heart is beating faster than normal. Not long ago, I was standing in the mirror talking to myself. I'm not feeling so good. My chest is getting tight. My health is still not one hundred percent. Somebody needs to tell him to stop telling my business.

Everyone in church is looking at me and whispering back and forth. Little kids are pointing their fingers at me and laughing. This is too uncomfortable. Why am I sweating? This will be my last time coming to this church. I need to go.

Just as I started to get up, someone touched me on the shoulder. A soft voice spoke to me.

"Relax, it's ok. Whatever you are going through, all you need to do is pray on it. God can fix anything."

She put her arms around me and told me everything would be ok. It's the usher I was talking to at the front door. She put my mind at ease for the moment.

I'm thinking maybe it's time for me to make an exit. My eyes are starting to tear up, and I don't want her to see me cry. I tried to turn my head away from her but before I could stand up, she wiped my face with a tissue and I noticed the tears in her eyes. She feels my pain also. We connected on a personal level right away. I have only felt like this about one woman, Kara. I can't explain.

* * * * *

Qualities of A Good Woman

Pastor finally dismissed church. I'm talking to this pretty lady again. Right when she was about to tell me her name, my Uncle Jessie walked up and stood next to me. Putting his arm around me he said,

"Son, she might be a relative."

This beautiful woman looked at me and I looked at her in disbelief. She slowly walked away. She didn't even say goodbye. This incident reminds me of my high school days. Every girl that I brought home to meet my parents ended up being a relative. I remember my mother saying,

"She's your cousin, Kory."

Then my mother would go on to explain the family tree. Déjà vu'!

Uncle Jessie thought it was funny, but hell I didn't. So, I asked him,

"Where is the best place to find a good woman?"

Seeing that I was serious he looked at me and answered, "The best place to find a good woman is in college. Nephew, let me explain. This may sound judgmental."

"In college, you can interact with a woman and learn a lot of things about her. You can learn information without falling too deep into a relationship. You need to know this information to decide if she is the one. There are some important things you need to look for. Number one is personality. Is she a nice woman and a likable person? Does she have a lot of friends, and what are they like? Is she comfortable reading a book, or does she have to be in the company of others?"

"Be sure to offer her a drink. Some women change personalities when they get a little alcohol in them. Alcohol brings the fool out of some women. And if by chance she drinks more than you do, run away from her as fast as you can. I hate to hear a woman call herself a bad bitch. That normally means she's a crazy, drama queen, dope-smoking, cussing loud mouth."

"Number two is morals. Faith, family and career should be on the top of her list. A woman who is beautiful, sexy and is known for being a free spirit, will break your heart. This type of woman normally has a lot of male friends or baby daddies. She dresses provocatively and has problems with commitment. There's a chance she may be bisexual. She likes to be seen. But the one woman that gets on my nerves, is the woman who chases after preachers. I don't know why they do it. Maybe they think having sex with preachers will get them in heaven."

"Number three is goals. Ask a potential mate what her goals are in life. If she says, 'I want to live my life doing what I want to do when I want to do it,' there is a good chance she is a stripper or a video girl. Never fall in love with either of the two. She is not relationship material. She's always on the go, and she will fight you. She will also have sex for money."

"If she is making bad grades in class, that means she's not motivated. A woman must want something in life besides a new sports car. An ambitious woman is a desirable choice. You want a woman who will encourage her man to be the best he can be. Stay away from a woman who spends money foolishly, and every time you see her, she wants you to give her some money. You go to the club, and she meet you at the door talking about, 'buy me a drank,' always begging."

"When a man's money falls short, a woman should step in and pick up the slack willingly. But there are some women who believe that if a man's salary cannot match her salary, then the man is not a potential husband. As a result, an alienation between man and woman is created. Some women do not recognize the potential of a good man."

"Also, beware of the woman with everything fake. You know what I mean, Kory, fake life, personality, hair, nails, boobs, and buttocks. There are a lot of fake people in this world. Try to make the right choice. Oh yeah, one more thing…this works both ways. A good woman is looking for the same qualities in a man. So, whenever you decide to go back to school, keep these things in mind. Prepare yourself for a great life, son. Take your cousin with you."

"Where is Wayne, Uncle Jessie?"

Uncle Jessie shook his head and shrugged his shoulders.

"I don't know, Kory. He's hanging out with some girl lately. Of course, that is not a terrible thing. He finally narrowed the women in his life down to one. He has been bringing her to Sunday dinner."

Uncle Jessie looks confused.

"So, who is the lucky lady, Unk?"

"Well, Kory, I don't remember her name, but she is a beautiful, dark chocolate woman."

Without hesitation, I replied, "Toni. Is her name, Toni, Unk?"

Uncle Jessie scratched his head and wrinkled his face.

"You know, Kory, I believe he did say her name was Toni or Tommie. She is very pretty. I am so glad for

my son. Invite him to go to college, Kory. I got to go.
See you next week, son."

"Ok, Uncle Jessie. I will see you next week."

* * * * *

New Beginnings

Leaving church, I am filled with optimism. My life is turning around. People who care about me are saying the same thing, *work your steps*. Reading the book Aunt Jackie gave me is weighing heavy on my mind.

Finally, I read the book, *12 Steps*. It took a while to finish reading and understanding the information. Seeing life the way God planned it, is becoming clearer each day. Everything is beginning to make sense. Every test that I pass makes me a stronger and better man. My daily routine of exercise and prayer has helped me to change into the man I always knew I could be.

The high or sense of consciousness that I am feeling at this moment has never surfaced in my life until now. This level of awareness was only an occasional thought hidden somewhere in the back of my mind. It finally gets a chance to excel. In short, I had a lightbulb moment. Taking this giant step will help strengthen me and land me in the place that I am destined to be. I graduated from the streets, if that's possible. Then I landed on the front lawn of the unavoidable place called college. It's an epiphany.

Staying focused and completing the task at hand was the problem I had the last time I was in college. It was too easy for me to quit and walk away. This time, I will complete my studies and do something with my life. Staying away from negativity is a priority. I have fallen behind, and all my positive-minded friends have moved on to discover heaven on earth. I need to make a life for me and my kids.

Now is the right time to call my girls and tell them the good news.

"Hello, how are my baby girls doing?"

"Hi Daddy, hi Daddy. We're doing ok."

Alicia replied, "How are you, Daddy?"

I can tell Alicia is not happy with the living conditions.

"Daddy is fine, baby. I wanted to tell my girls the good news."

Alicia asked, "What news, Daddy?

"Are you coming to get us, Daddy?"

I answered,

"Alicia, I know you miss mama. I miss mama, too. Yes, I am coming to get you. That's not all. The good news is I'm going back to college, and I'm getting my life together. I promise I will be the best dad you have ever seen. You just wait and see."

Alicia replied, "Wow, that's great Daddy! You sound excited. And you can finally get the job you always wanted."

"My teacher, Mr. Gregory, said that the goal in life is to be self-employed."

I thought for a minute and then answered Alicia.

"That's a great idea, Alicia, and I will definitely consider the possibilities of being self-employed. Thanks, baby! Well, I just turned into the parking lot at Progressive College. I'm running late, so I got to go. See you later, girls. Tell your grandmother I will be by after I get out of class."

Both girls answered, "Ok, Daddy. I love you, Daddy."

"I love you, too, Kelsi."

"I love you, Daddy."

I love you, too, Alicia."

"Alicia, we will work this out together, ok?"

"Ok, Daddy."

"Bye, Daddy,"

"Bye, Daddy."

"Bye, babies."

Wow! What an enjoyable conversation I had with my little girls, but now I am late to class. Now that Kara is out of town, I must step up my parenting skills. I park my truck, hurry across the parking lot and get the last remaining seat in the class. The teacher started giving his lecture and received a phone call. He instructed the class to take a short break while he went to the Dean's office.

Everyone in class walked out in the hall and waited for the teacher to return. Moving slow, I stood in the doorway of the classroom.

"Hi, Kory."

Someone standing behind me is speaking to me. I recognized the voice, so I turned around to see if it was her. It's the Usher that I met at church.

"Hello beautiful lady. You are the angel I met at church Sunday."

She smiled as I kissed her hand. The two of us made a connection that we both knew was real. This connection could potentially bond us for years to come.

After class, I walked her to her car and I finally got a chance to ask her.

"What is your name?"

She laughed and said,

"I didn't think you were going to ask me. My name is Angelle (Unjell)."

I told her, "I've never heard a name like that before it's…it's…pretty."

I laughed. She replied,

"What's so funny? Are you making fun of my name?"

I responded,

"Noo…noo. I was just thinking. How will I remember such a pretty name? I know, it's like Jell-O that's not jelled. Yeah, yeah, that's it. Liquid Jell-O."

We both laughed like we had known each other all our lives. We were comfortable as she hugged me and opened the door to her car. After she cranked the car, she boldly said,

"Oh yeah, tell your Uncle my mama said I am not his daughter and he can kiss her you know what."

"What, my uncle, Angelle?"

"Yes, your uncle. He may want to avoid my mama for a while. I told her what he said about us being relatives and she did not like it."

I said,

"Oookkk Angelle, I'll make sure my uncle gets the message." Thinking to myself, in fact, I will be sure to let him know, you are the one for me.

* * * * *

Kara is Back

The next two years, we were always together. Angelle frequently reminds me that I don't look at her the way I look at Kara's picture. I try to explain that my history with Kara goes back to my childhood. We also have two daughters together. Two daughters who miss their mother. We just need more time to develop a relationship like I had with Kara.

As a couple, we are getting better every day. Our personal journeys put us at the center of our lives. We were like two kids playing in the park and never wanting to go home. We can and often finished each other's sentences. Angelle is also a good cook. My daughters love her. Life is so good. I thought I was in love before, but now I know what love is supposed to feel like. Kara told me to find a good woman to raise our daughters. Angelle is the one. We are making plans to marry after we graduate from college. The wedding will be next fall. Angelle needs time to get wedding plans together. She has been doing a lot of shopping with her mother. I don't know why it takes so long. She has already chosen a location for the wedding. I think she said the reception will be outside somewhere. I'm not sure. But she is truly a blessing to me.

I just need to chill. This whole wedding thing is stressing me out. The doorbell rings as my eyes are closing. I get to the door as quickly as I can. Opening the front door, there stands my first love.

Kara's black silky hair is longer than before. It extends to her waist. Her hat tilts to one side with a band the same color as her eyes. Opening her floor length sweater, she displayed a pair of faded blue jean shorts. Her blouse opened down the middle to show off her shapely abdomen. The September breeze makes her body very inviting. She is more beautiful than ever before. I opened the storm door, and she jumped in my arms. She gave me a welcome-home kiss. We couldn't stop touching each other. The girls jumped up and down like their favorite team had just scored a touchdown. We all cried and had a group hug. It has been a long time since we were all together. Kara is home.

My wife is clinging to me like she never has in the past. She is talking and crying at the same time.

"Things have calmed down considerably so we can be a family again, Kory. It feels good to be home. I missed my family. Turn around so I can jump on your back."

We both laughed and played horsey running through the house. Kelsi and Alicia joined in with us.

"Let's go in the backyard and play with the dogs, Daddy."

"Ok, let's go outside and play, girls."

"Yeahhh. Get in the pool, Mama. I can swim all the way across now Mama. Watch."

"Ok, Kelsi. Be careful."

"Ok, Mama."

"Watch your sister while I talk to Daddy Alicia."

"Ok, Mama. I'll watch, Kelsi."

"Kory Henderson, sit down and talk to me. What is going on in your life?"

"Well, Kara Henderson, I followed your instructions."

Kara looked at me with question.

"What instructions, Kory?"

With a serious look on my face,

"Don't you remember, Kara? You told me to find a woman suitable enough to raise our daughters. For the last two years, that is what I have been doing. I found someone, Kara."

The look on Kara's face said you are not marrying anybody.

"Well, Kory, you have to break up with her because I am back to stay. I can take care of my own family."

"I know you can Kara, but what about her? She is really a nice woman. The girls like her too."

"What is her name, Kory? Do I know her?"

"Her name is Angelle. I don't think you know her."

"Kory, I'm back. Find a way to fix things. You look disappointed. Aren't you glad to see me?"

I replied,

"Of course, I am glad to see you. I think about you all the time. But it may not be that simple, Kara. It will take some time. I don't want to hurt her feelings. You must be patient, Kara. I will handle it. Don't you do anything to hurt her feelings. Ok?"

"Ok, Kory. You handle it."

"Ok, I will continue the relationship, Kara. When the time is right, I will break it off."

"So, let's go somewhere and celebrate my homecoming, Kory."

"Ok, Kara. What do you have in mind?"

"I want to have fun and eat some great food, Kory."

"Kara, I know where we can do both. Jack Binion's Steak House."

Kara got excited.

"Yes, Kory! I haven't been to the casino in two years. That is a great idea. Let's make reservations for next weekend, Kory. For now, I want to hold my daughters and never let them go. I thought about them every day for the last two years."

"Ok, Kara, I'll call."

The following Friday, we head to the casino. We dropped the girls off at Kara's mom's house. Both of us were excited. We sang along with the radio all the way to Bossier City, Louisiana. Kara's kiss is magnificent. I almost swerved off the road a couple of times.

"Kara, you're going to make me wreck my truck."

She looked at me and laughed.

"Kory, I really missed you. It feels so good to be home. I am so excited about us. This time around, we will make our marriage work."

"Yes, we will, Kara."

"Kory, hold my hand, and don't ever let it go."

"We made it here just in time, Kara. Our reservation is at seven fifteen."

Kara took off her seatbelt and sat on her knees. She's bouncing around in the truck like she is on a trampoline. She's looking out of the window like she is afraid she might miss seeing something.

"Hurry and find a parking space, Kory. I'm starving."

Kara was glowing, so I sat and admired my wife. She stopped looking out of the window and looked at me. She spoke in a soft, bedroom voice.

"What are you looking at, Kory?"

I replied,

"I missed you, Kara. I missed your long beautiful hair, your soft skin, your tiny waist and" …

Before I could finish my sentence, Kara straddled me. Then we shared a moment.

"Ok, let's go in, Kara."

Walking toward the entrance, I noticed a car that looked familiar.

"Kara, if I didn't know any better, I would swear this Camry belongs to Angelle. No, it couldn't be. She's a good, church girl."

Kara looks at me like she can't believe I said that.

"Kory, she's human just like we are. What does she look like anyway? I haven't ever seen her."

"Well, Kara since you asked. I have a picture of her in my cell phone." We stepped inside and waited for the elevator.

"This is her. She's about five feet six and thick in all the right places. Her hair is black and about shoulder length. Her skin is smooth and unblemished. Her waist line is small like yours, and she wears big hoop ear rings. All her body parts are real, no augmentations. Her smile brightens up a room. Other than that, she's normal."

Kara was looking disappointed.

"Well, thank you, Kory. I feel better already. Thank you very much. Why are you laughing, Kory?"

Hugging Kara, I explained.

"Kara, you know I have good taste in women. I chose you, didn't I? Why are you laughing, Kara?"

"Kory, men don't choose women. Women choose men. That's the way of the world."

We both laughed.

"Whatever, Kara. The elevator door is opening."

Getting off the elevator we walked through the hotel. We took pictures on the beautiful cars that the casino was giving away. We walked past the club and the band was playing Marvin Gaye, "Let's Get It On." We danced a while before going to Jack Binion's.

"Kara, we worked up one hell of an appetite in the parking garage."

Kara walked with both of her arms around my waist and looking up in my eyes.

"Yes, we did Kory Henderson. I am starved."

The maître d' greeted us at the entrance of the restaurant.

"Hi, welcome to Jack Binion's Steak House. Do you have a reservation?

"Hi, Henderson reservations for two."

She responded.

"Oh, yes sir, right this way."

Kara was all smiles.

"Kory, this is nice. I love the ambience. The light is down low. We are sitting in a booth overlooking the water. I never want to leave this place."

Looking over the wine list, I tried to impress Kara.

"How about some wine for the lovely lady? Why kind would you like, Kara?"

She tried to be nice and let me choose.

"I don't know, Kory. You choose the wine."

"I don't know either, Kara. I buy my wine at The Big Wall Store. How about I order some Arbor Mist, Merlot?"

She chuckled.

"They probably don't have that one, Kory."

We laughed out loud.

Sitting across the table Kara grabbed my hand and kissed it. I kissed her hand as well. Her shoulders pushed upward. She tapped her feet on the floor with joy.

"Is that a tear I see in your eye, Kara?"

She smiled as I wiped it.

"Yes, it is, Kory. It's the same tear you have in your eye? Kory, this reminds me of the times when we were in high school. We used to go to Battee's Bar-b-que for lunch. One winter, the windshield on your car was frozen. You could not see how to drive. There was one clear spot by the rearview mirror. I told you which way to go. We drove there and back without having an accident. You trusted me one hundred percent. I will never forget those days."

"You are so right, Kara. Maybe we should order a smoked link sandwich and a bag of barbeque Fritos with a Nu-grape soda."

We laughed.

"I don't think so, Kory. I want a big steak, twice baked potato with corn and shrimp macque choux."

"Yeah, that sounds good. I believe I will have the same, Kara. Good choice."

"Kory, I am having a wonderful time. Thanks for bringing me here."

We held hands the whole time we were in the restaurant.

"Kara, you are so welcome."

The waitress brought our food, and we ate every bite.

"When we finish eating, we will go into the casino."

"Yes, I can't wait, Kory. I am so excited."

"Me too, Kara. Before we leave this weekend, we really need to have a talk. Here let me wipe the food off your mouth, baby."

"Yeah, I know we do, Kory. We can't just act like nothing ever happened. We need to talk about it and get past it. You have some food on your mouth too, Kory. Let me kiss it clean for you."

"Alright, Kara, don't start something you can't finish. We might not make it into the casino."

We both laughed.

"Kory, if I start it, I promise you, I will finish it. Do you see the look in my eyes?"

Laughing at Kara,

"I think I see it, Kara. Kara, you are a totally different person. I remember times in the past when you would not listen to me. Now, I feel like I am your husband."

"I know, Kory. Time has a way of changing things. Time also heals old wounds. We have been through some things that changed my perception of life. We are finally moving in the right direction."

* * * * *

Kory Contemplates

"Let's go into the casino and have some fun."

"Let's go."

Kara moves around the casino playing different machines. I finally find her to see if she is having fun.

"Kory, we have played for an hour or so and haven't won anything. I'm tired of playing on this floor. I'm going upstairs."

"Ok Kara. If I don't win something within the next hour, I will join you."

"Ok, Kory."

Humm, I wonder if I can remember how to play craps. Let me google my notes and study for a minute. How hard can it be? I walked around all the crap tables and payed attention. Nervous, I decided to take a chance. Let's do it. Time to play.

Angelle and Kara

"Excuse me, I didn't mean to bump into you. Well, actually I did mean to bump into you."

The lady looked at me as if she was surprised.

"You're Angelle, aren't you?"

Angelle was surprised that she had been recognized.

"Kory showed me your picture. He also thought he recognized your car in the parking garage. He really didn't look too close." I first saw you in the restaurant. I didn't mention it to Kory because I wasn't sure. But when I saw you peeping from around the slot machine, I knew it was you."

Angelle is starting to get angry.

"Well since you know who I am, who are you?"

I worked my neck and gave her the sister girl look.

"I'm Kara, Kory's wife."

Angelle looked downward and started to cry.

"You're his wife?"

"Yes, I came back home last week."

Angelle tried to collect her emotions before speaking.

"Kory said you left and didn't know if you would ever return."

With a serious look on my face, "That's true, Angelle. But I am back. Kory and I are celebrating my return. I must say Angelle, I don't understand your reaction. Instead of crying, I would be mad as hell. If I saw my fiancée with another woman, I would be furious."

A man walks up and stands next to Angelle.

"Angelle, who is your friend?"

Angelle wiped her tears.

"Oh, Morris this is Kara."

Morris speaks.

"Hello, Kara, how are you?"

"Fine, thank you, Morris. I need to find my husband. He's in here somewhere. The two of you enjoy your evening."

I turned and walked away. I need to find Kory before he comes upstairs.

* * * * *

Kory Shoots Craps

"Waitress can I get a double shot of Crown Royal. Keep them coming. Dealer, can I have six hundred dollars in chips please?"

The dealer looked at me and smiled.

"Yes, you can, sir. Place your bets, everyone."

"Thank you, waitress. That was fast. Keep them coming."

I dropped my money on the table.

"Give me $50 on six and $50 on eight."

The stick man replied.

"Roll the dice."

"Six wins. Place your bets."

I respond, "Let it ride."

The dice is rolled again. The stick man responds, "Eight wins. Place your bets."

I'm feeling pretty good now. I raised my bet.

"Stick man, give me a $100 world."

The Stick man replied, "Roll the dice. Three wins."

I am jumping for joy.

"Yes, I won again!"

Stick man said,

"Place your bets."

I told him, "let it ride."

Stick man said, "Roll dice."

The dealer says, "Eleven wins."

"I don't believe it. I won again."

Once again, the stick man says, "Place your bets. Roll the dice. Two wins."

"I don't believe it. I should have been playing dice all along."

Again, the stick man says place your bets.

I shouted out, "Let it ride!"

Everyone around the table was laughing and cheering me on. The dealer said,

"Seven."

The dealers wipe the table clean. I responded, "Hold up, sir. Where is my money? I didn't lose."

Everyone laughed. The dealer responded,

"A seven was rolled. You lost your money."

Trying not to get upset, I spoke respectfully.

"No, I didn't lose. My bet was a world. On a world bet, a seven roll is a push."

Everyone laughed. Now, I am pissed.

"Damn it, I didn't lose! Where is my money?"

The Box lady gave me a go to hell look.

"You lost the bet, man."

I replied, "No, I didn't lose the bet. You don't know how to play."

She replied, "I been playing for a long time. You lost the bet. Don't get your ass put out of the casino."

Security walked up, stood next to me.

"This is not street dice. Play or get out, fella."

"Hell, no," I stated.

"It's apparent that you all don't know the rules. Call the pit boss, please? You are cheating me out of my money."

Security grabbed me by the arm and was about to escort me out.

The pit boss walked up. The dealers told him what happened.

"Mr. Moretti, this guy rolled a seven and thinks he won."

I replied.

"I didn't say I won. I said it's a push. I placed a world bet. If a seven is rolled on a world bet, it's a push. I don't win, and I don't lose."

Everyone around the table laughed. Mr. Moretti explained.

"A world bet is a rare bet. Most people don't even know what it is. The player is right. Rolling a seven on a world bet is a push."

The other players around the table were amazed at what Mr. Moretti said.

"Sir, what is your name?"

I answered, "My name is Henderson."

Mr. Moretti replied, "I apologize, Mr. Henderson. Give Mr. Henderson his money back."

The crowd is cheering but confused. They are all talking. *How you roll a seven and don't lose your money?* The pit boss walked away. I could not help myself. I had to rub it in.

"Well, I guess he told y'all. May I please have my money?" I may have laughed a little too much.

"What's the matter casino employees? You all look confused. Let me guess. You don't remember how much I won. Well damn. You all can't count, can you? Maybe I will let you use my fingers.' How many of y'all graduated from junior high school?"

Laughing and drinking my Crown Royal, they got pissed off. The box lady responded.

"We will give you your money, Mr. Henderson."

"Ok, lady. You all hurry up with my eight thousand dollars. Where is my damn drink? This might take a while."

"Anybody want a Snickers bar?"

The people around the table laughed.

"As long as you all are taking, I want fifteen percent interest on my money. Where is that damn drink?"

One of the players walked closer to me.

"Hey, man, be cool. These Italians don't play that. They will kick your butt."

I looked at him like he was crazy.

"Kick whose butt? They need to get my ten thousand dollars. Looks like they can't count, two, five, sixteen. What school did they go to?"

Kara walked up and stood next to me.

"Oh, Kory, there you are. I was waiting for you to come upstairs. I didn't win anything, so I came back down to check on you. I thought you might like a Heineken."

"Yeah, I could use another Heineken. I won, baby! Now, I need my damn money."

"Kory, lower your voice and stop hitting the table. You are drunk. We need to go, Kory."

"Where is the bathroom, Mr. Dealer? Kara, they need a calculator because they can't count. I'm not feeling so good. Earrrrr, oh my stomach."

"Hold your head down, Kory. You are throwing up on the crap table. Sir, I'm sorry. My husband is drunk. I'm taking him to the room."

"Wait a damn…minute Kara. I want my damn money. They owe me twenty thousand dollars. I got a bad headache, Kara. Somebody put something in my drink. The room is spinning."

"Stop cussing, Kory. Sir, I am sorry for my husband's behavior. Can I come back and get the money?"

"Ma'am, write your information and room number down on this paper. I will have someone bring it up to you."

"Thank you. Ok, that's it. Come on, Kory. Let's go to the room."

Kory and I walked out of the casino and headed to the elevator.

* * * * *

Kara confronts Kory's Addiction

"Kara, I think we need to go to another casino. Let's go check out Sam's Town Casino. Come on Kara. You say you didn't win anything at all upstairs, Kara? You were up there for quite a while. Anyway, let's go to Sam's Town."

"I don't think so, Kory."

"Where is the waitress?"

"You are talking really loud, Kory. It's four o'clock in the morning. The waitress has gone home. Let's go to bed. I'm tired. I can't stop yawning. How much have you had to drink Kory?"

The two of us stood in front of the elevator.

"Well, Kara, I think I have had one or two beers, hahahahaha."

"Kory, you're drunk."

"Kara, I am not drunk. I can hold my liquor, hahahahaha. I can't keep my eyes open, but I can hold my liquor. Help me inside the elevator."

"Kory, I think we should eat breakfast in the morning and go back home. We don't need to stay another day. I have had enough casino for one day."

The next morning, we woke up late.

"Wake up, Kory. We need to check out of this room. If we stay pass 11:00 they will charge us for another day. Get dressed so we can go."

"Ok, Kara, I'm coming. Are we all packed?"

"Yes, Kory. Get the bag and let's go. Come on walk faster. Hold the elevator, please. Thank you. Come on, Kory, there is just enough room for the two of us. Turn the luggage sideways so the door will close."

"Ok, Kara, going down please."

The elevator door opens on the first floor, and people start to exit.

"Let's go Kory. Come on, let's go, Kory. Why are you stopping? Kara, you go to the front desk and check out. I'll be there in a minute."

"What are you doing, Kory? Why are you standing in front of the elevator with your arms folded?"

Out walks Angelle. Her friend is walking a few steps ahead of her.

"Well, well, well. If it's not Angelle. The good church girl. Funny meeting you here, fiancé. I recognized the short, bouncy, curly hairstyle when I stepped onto the elevator. It looked like you were trying to hide."

I moved in between Kory and Angelle.

"Kory, please don't do this here. Just leave her alone."

Kory looked over my head and made eye contact with Angelle. Angelle starts crying.

"Kory, I'm sorry."

Angelle's friend turns around and addresses her.

"Angelle, what's going on, honey?"

He put his arm around Angelle.

"Why are you crying?"

"Morris, I'm sorry. This is Kory."

Morris replies, "Kory, the ex-boyfriend? Oh, ok. Kory, why are you making Angelle cry? She's my woman now. We are getting married."

People are walking between us entering the elevator.

Kory's brown face turned purple as a grape. I can tell he is ready to fight. Angelle turned toward Morris and shouted out.

"I'm not your woman, Morris! You don't want to work. I'm not marrying any man who doesn't work."

Morris responded.

"Angelle, I am a preacher. That's my job."

Kory could not keep quiet.

"You a preacher, and you don't have to work. There are several preachers on my job who work sixty hours a week. Most of them are pastors. What makes you so special that you don't have to work? Your ass is just sorry as hell."

Morris responded in an angry voice.

"Don't you cuss me. I am a man of God. God takes care of me."

Kory reached in his pocket.

"I'll take care of you, partner."

I grabbed his arm before he could bring his hand out. Angelle screamed.

"Kory, no! Please don't do anything stupid."

The crowd scattered. Somebody called security.

Kory looked at Angelle like he wanted to slap her.

"You called me stupid? I will kill the both of you. I pushed Kory against the wall.

"No, Kory! Please stop. Please, Kory! I'm begging you."

Kory responded.

"A man that doesn't work shouldn't eat. You are a poor example of a man. You need a job with benefits. Set a good example for your kids. How do you call yourself a man if you don't work and take care of your family? You are having sex with women in the congregation. You are right about one thing. God will take care of you."

Morris had to have the last word.

"You can say whatever you want to ex-boyfriend."

Morris walked closer to Kory and laughed in his face.

"I had her last night."

I could not hold Kory back any longer.

"I will whoop your jackleg ass."

Kory beat the hell out of Morris. Security came and broke up the fight. We hurried to the car

and headed west on Interstate 20.

* * * * *

Rehab

Driving home, Kara didn't have much to say.

"What's on your mind, Kara?"

Kara looked at me out of the corner of her eye. She made a sighing noise blowing wind from her nose.

"I'm trying to figure out how to fix this, Kory. Last night, you were very drunk. I have never seen you drink so much liquor. They were about to throw us out of the casino. You said some things to the casino employees that you should not have said. I was embarrassed to say the least. But I love you, and I will always be here for you. We are the parents of two beautiful daughters. They need two good parents to raise them."

"What are you trying to say, Kara? Am I not good enough to raise my own children? Are you leaving again? Damn, Kara. I can't seem to get this family thing right."

Kara grabbed my hand. She put my hand against her neck and laid her head on it.

"Kory, I know you want to be a good father. First, you need to be a good man. You need to go to rehab. Your substance abuse problem must be addressed and resolved. Don't look at me like that, Kory. Get that wrinkle out of your forehead. You are messing up that handsome face."

We laughed.

"Yeah, Kara. I guess you are right. I need some professional help. When I get to work, I will check with human resources."

"No, Kory, the people on your job will be all in our business. You can use my company insurance if you want more privacy. It's up to you."

"Humm, you are probably right, Kara. There are a lot of messy people working on my assembly line. You handle it, baby."

Kara has a big smile on her face.

"You haven't called me baby in a while, Kory. I will take care of you, Kory. I promise."

It took about two weeks for me to get into rehab. It's important for me to grasp all the usable information that is offered in the center. This has got to work. My family's future depends on it. We got in the car. Kara wanted to drive.

"Come on, Kory, let's go."

"Ok, Kara, I had to get my suitcase and lock the back door."

"I'll drive, Kory."

I got in on the passenger's side of her SUV.

"This is different. I'm not used to you driving, Kara."

Excited about me going to rehab, Kara reached over and hugged me.

"Close your eyes and get some rest, Kory. I got this."

I looked over at Kara and smiled. Then I let my seat back and closed my eyes.

"This is relaxing, Kara. Houston, here we come."

Twenty minutes later, she stopped. The back door opened.

"What up, kinfolk? Let the trunk up, Kara."

I opened my eyes, "Wayne, where are you going?"

Wayne and Toni climbed into the back seat.

"Kory, I guess they didn't tell you. I just found out myself last night. We going to rehab."

Kara and Toni both laughed and looked away from me. I looked at Kara over my sunglasses.

"Kara, not telling all of the information is the same as telling a lie."

She stopped laughing. She turned her head toward me and caressed my head with her hand.

"Kory, you're right. I'm sorry. But I didn't know how to tell you."

Disappointed in Kara, I explained.

"Just tell the truth, Kara. That is all I ask."

"Ok, you are right, Kory."

I turned around and looked at Toni.

"What are you laughing at, Toni? How long have you and Kara been planning this trip?"

"Kara called me a week ago, Kory. It sounded like a good idea to me. You and Wayne seem to get into trouble together. Why not clean up together? Don't be mad, Kory. Kara and I want what's best for our men."

Looking away from Toni and looking at Kara, I responded.

"Really?"

Wayne finished putting the bags in the trunk. Kara got out of the car and walked around to the passenger side.

She had a slight grin on her face as she opened my door.

"Ok, Kory, you can drive."

In a sarcastic way, I begin to express my feeling. With a wrinkled forehead, I answered.

"Yeah, relax, Kory. Close your eyes and go to sleep. I got this, Kory. Yeah, right."

Kara laughed and pulled me out of the car by my arms. Standing on the tips of her toes, she gave me a big kiss.

"Oh, Kory, you know I love you."

Looking down at my beautiful wife, I responded.

"Yeah, I know, Kara."

We made it to Houston in a matter of hours. We got out of the car and said our goodbyes.

"Kory, call home every chance you get."

"Ok, I will, Kara."

"Give me a hug, Kory. I love you. Make this rehab work for me, you and our daughters, Kory. It makes me happy to know that you want to change your life."

Wayne and Toni are also saying their goodbyes. Closing the car door, Kara rolled the window down still talking.

"Let me know when I can come visit, Kory. I'm sure the girls will want to see you."

Kara and Toni drove away as Wayne and I stood watch.

Wayne and I checked in and met some of the other patients.

"Wayne, do you see anybody you know?"

Wayne had an unsure look on his face.

"Well Kory, you know I know people. I might know a couple of these knuckle heads. I'll wait and see if they know me first."

We both laughed.

"Yeah, you're right, Wayne. Some of these crackheads look familiar. But I don't want to put myself out there too soon. They need to acknowledge me before I say something."

We are still laughing.

"Hey Wayne."

A female from across the room recognized Wayne. Now we are laughing hard.

"Yeah Wayne, you said you know people."

"Come on Kory. Let's go see who she is."

"I'm right behind you, Wayne."

Now everyone is looking at us.

"Wayne."

People are shouting his name all over the center.

"Wayne, this is like an episode of the television show *Cheers*. We walked in and everyone knows your name. You might be getting around a little too much."

Wayne, shaking his head and looking downward, he spoke in disbelief.

"Well, damn. Everyone knows my name. This is like a class reunion. But it's more like a night-life reunion. I met you all at places that I should not have been. This is proof that I need to change my life. I guess I am in the right place."

Wayne was looking sad. I put my arm around his shoulder.

"Wayne don't cry. We came here for help."

The counselors called a group meeting. All the patients introduced themselves. Today is the first day of drug rehab for all the patients in attendance. The counselor said tomorrow we will do assessments. We go to sleep early and get up early. Wayne and I shared a room.

We got up early the next morning. Neither Wayne nor I have ever had a drug assessment. We were surprised to find out what happens. The first day of rehab, we got high. They got the good stuff. Several of the patients tried to slip drugs into their underwear. The counselors caught them and removed the drugs. All the patients went to their bedroom. The rooms had twin beds. Wayne and I sat and talked for a while.

"Kory, I didn't know we were going to get high. I'll be damned. They got the good, brown looking cocaine. We might not ever leave this place. Kory, I am moving to Houston. This place is off the chain. Hell, let's go outside and smoke this Snoop Dawg I smuggled out."

We laughed, holding our sides.

"Wayne, you are crazy as hell. But I admit. I have never been this high. This place must have a cartel connection."

The next day, we started group therapy.

"Kory, if I sit in one more meeting I'm going to sleep."

Looking at Wayne, I scratched my head.

"Wayne, you were sleep. Now we are taking a break, so you can wake up. Everyone was looking and laughing at you snore. You sound like a wild hog."

Wayne was embarrassed.

"Kory, I was not snoring. Why you laughing?"

Shaking my head at Wayne,

"Right, Wayne. Let's walk out by the pool."

"Anyway, you missed my confession Wayne. I shared a moment when I was doing wrong. I did wrong, and I knew it was wrong. But you were sleep, and you missed it."

Wayne looked at me with his head tilted to the side like my dogs do.

"Kory, I am trying to narrow it down to one incident you would confess to. You know the two of us have been involved in a whole lot of trouble. It is a wonder we are not dead or in jail."

"That's the truth, Wayne. But think back a couple of years ago."

"Hum, Kory, you got me scratching my head on this one."

"Ok, Wayne, I talked about the time the two of us drove to Austin."

"Kory, what? No, you didn't. You better hope nobody in this rehab center knows your wife. Man, I don't believe you told that story. Dang, I missed it."

"Wayne, think back. Remember how it all started?"

* * * * *

Lake Palestine

We ride several miles on Highway 155 South until we reach the first liquor store in Coffee City. On this rare occasion, the liquor store is full of girls in bikinis. As usual, Wayne knows half the women in the store. He is like the ambassador of East Texas. He knows somebody everywhere he goes. Wayne is hugging, kissing and touching all the women in the store. We are walking around the store like we own the place.

The store manager is looking at us like we are about to steal something. He wants us to make a purchase and leave. I can't decide what to buy. Strolling down the aisle reading the labels on the bottles, I bump into a beautiful female. Bending down reading the labels on the lower shelves with her girlfriend, she stands and looks at me. She is about 5'2" and 130 pounds. Immediately, I apologize.

"Oh, I'm sorry. I didn't mean to bump you. Are you ok?"

She is wearing blue jean booty shorts with horizontal rips. Her skin is showing in between the rips. Her stilettos are the same color as her hair. Her body looks like she spends a lot of time in the gym. She must be the squat queen because her lower body is thick and muscular. Her bikini top only covers her nipples and everything else is exposed. I asked her,

"I didn't hurt you, did I?"

She laughed as if she knew I did it on purpose.

"Oh no, I'm fine. It didn't hurt."

So, I asked her, "Can I do it again?"

Now, she's really laughing. A guy walks up and stands next to her looking me up and down. He stands about 6'5" and 350 pounds of solid muscle. I'm thinking to myself, *where in the hell did Debo come from?*

"You got a new friend, Marisa?"

She started speaking in Spanish and then answered.

"No, we just bumped into each other, Alarico."

Marisa's girlfriend laughed. Marisa looked at her,

"Hush, Erika."

Now Alarico is really checking me out. A wrinkle has formed in the middle of his forehead, and his eyebrows pushed upward.

"Yeah, I know that move, my friend. It's all good. My Marisa is beautiful and sexy. All the guys want her, but she belongs to me."

Then he gave me some dap. I thought he was about to punch me, so I gave him a little head fake. I really need that drink now. Cognac sounds good. I walked away from the three of them, headed to the cash register and paid for my liquor. I waited in the car while Mr. Ambassador was still shaking hands.

* * * * *

Pool Party

Finally, we are driving back down FM 2661. Relieved to be away from the gladiator boyfriend, I can relax. We will be at my house in a minute. Then out of nowhere, Wayne turns into The Exclusive Villager Resort. I am like,

"Where are you going?"

He has a little sly grin on his face talking about,

"They are having a pool party, dawg. Did you see all those fine bodies in the liquor store? It was like the United Nations, all colors and all flavors. We are about to strike gold. Also, they are having a beauty pageant somewhere in Dallas next weekend. I will be right there."

I took a deep breath and slowly released it.

"Wayne, we can't stay long. I need to get back home. You seem to have forgotten I am already in trouble with my wife."

"Kory, you right, you right. We are just stopping by for a minute and we out. You feel me?"

Hesitating, I replied,

"I feel you, Wayne." Let's go check out the United Nations pool party."

We both laughed because we kinfolk, and that is how we roll.

Driving up to the entrance of the resort, there is a closed gate that requires a pin number to enter. I look at Wayne and he tells me,

"No problem, I got this."

Wayne enters a pin number and the gate opens. Still looking at him, I shake my head, and we both laugh. I asked him,

"Wayne, where did you get a pin number?"

He responded,

"I know people. We are inside, cuz. Let's do this."

Driving through the gate down a long winding road, the music gets louder. There is a party going on in the middle of the day. We pull up and park at poolside. I recognize the song. It's "The Humpty Dance." The place is packed with women. There are women in the pool, on the grass, in the parking lot and in the cabins. There is a dance contest going on between sorority girls and strippers. The game is called 'twerk and shot.' Twerk for a shot of Patron. The place is turned up and lit. I talked and touched every woman at the party. The best part about the party was bumping into Marisa. Her boyfriend was somewhere drunk and passed out. Marisa and I talked and got comfortable with each other. Marisa's friend, Erika, told her,

"He's trouble."

Then Marisa and I slipped away into a dark corner by the lake away from the bright lights. The moon is shining a soft romantic glow. A picnic table is placed in the perfect spot. I pick her up by her waist and put her on the table. The table stands at just the right height. I tried to kiss her, but she resisted and turned her head. Everything seemed to change in my favor when the D.J. played a love song. The song was "Let's Love" by the Ohio Players. Softly, I sing the song to her. She could no longer resist. My manhood is standing solid and firm. She wrapped her legs around my waist and pulled me into her. She is calling me *Papi* in the sexiest bedroom voice I ever heard. Tonight, is Thanksgiving, Christmas, New Year, Fourth of July and my birthday all in one. She lit the candle on the cake, and I don't think it will be going out anytime soon.

There is a bright set of car lights coming toward us. It's Wayne.

"Kory, get in. Hurry up! Her boyfriend is coming down the hill through the woods."

Both of us were completely naked and in the act of making love. Marisa grabbed our clothes off the table and put them in between us. I tried to remove myself from her, but she squeezed a tight vacuum between us. I ran to the car with her legs still wrapped around me. She would not let go. I put the both of us in the back seat of the old school convertible and Wayne sped away. Marisa was hysterical.

"Please do not let him catch me. He tells me all the time that I am his property and if I cheat, he will kill me. His brother killed his wife for trying to leave him. The men in his family are very abusive toward their women."

Wayne looked back at Marisa and said,

"If you know your man is crazy, why the hell are you cheating?"

Marisa screamed, "I hate him. Please don't let him find me."

Wayne looked back at us again,

"Kory, you and your girl need to get dressed. You look like two dogs hung up. I'm just saying.

I need to let the top up on my car before we all get arrested."

* * * * *

Marisa

Marisa is a nice girl with negative influences in her life. She got mixed up with the wrong person early in life. I guess we are one in the same. Tonight, the right people are together. We talked and enjoyed each other's company all night long. I confessed to her.

"Marisa, women come and go in my life, and most of the time, I do not care one way or the other. You are the one woman that I would hate to lose. We connected immediately. The sex between us is off the chain. But sex is not what you need. You need help getting your life together. I want you to be happy. Tell me what you want me to do. Where is your family?"

Crying and smiling at the same time, she answered.

"My family lives in Harlingen, Texas. I also have an uncle who lives in Austin with his family. He said if I come to Austin, he can get me a job and help me get started with a new life. I'm thinking maybe that is the best thing for me. If I go back to Alarico, I am dead. Please, help me. Please."

Looking at Wayne in his rearview mirror, "Man, what do you think?"

He looked back in the mirror at me.

"Kory, you know I know people. I got a homeboy who lives in Austin. When we were kids back in my old neighborhood on Dargan Street, we were next door neighbors. We can crash at his house before we come back. Austin is a four-hour drive from here. I am game if you are, Kory."

"I am game, Wayne. Let's ride. I will pay for the gas."

Without thinking about the consequences of our journey, we ventured to Austin, Texas. Marisa relaxed and fell asleep in the same position as when we got in the car. Occasionally, she would wake up and continue what we started at the party. This by far is the best road trip I have ever experienced. She kept saying,

"Thank you, Papi. I will never forget you. When you bumped into me at the liquor store, I felt a positive exchange of energy. Something about you put my mind at ease and made me feel safe. It has been a long time since I have felt this way in the company of a man. Alarico would not let me voice my opinion. You are my property, he says. 'I own you.' It is a constant reminder every day. I have not felt loved since I moved away from my family. My mother used to cook breakfast on Saturday morning and my uncles, aunts and cousins would come over. We were a very close family. I want to feel that again."

Yawning and stretching, Marisa fell asleep.

My eyes won't stay shut. I close them, and they pop right back open. Considering the events that have taken place in the last 24 hours, a normal person would be sleep. There's a lot on my mind. My outlook on life is a big question mark. My direction is uncertain. I am living large on top of the world. At the same time, I have responsibilities that should have priority. Life can be so complicated. I am confused and unsure about the direction of my path from this point. I contemplate telling my wife. Marriage is the last thing on my mind right now. Having a child with someone does not necessarily qualify you for marriage. There is still a lot that I want to do with my life but now, I am a big baller. A big baller cannot be held down by one woman. All the beautiful women need a taste of Papi. We dropped Marisa off at her uncle's house and Wayne and I spent the night at his homeboy's house. The next morning, we headed back to Tyler.

"You missed a great story, Wayne."

Wayne shook his head.

"That wasn't a story, Kory. That came from a real place."

The two of us walked out of the building. We went down the steps by the swimming pool. Somebody recognized me.

"Kory. Kory? It is you."

She ran and jumped in my arms.

"Swirvae. Oh, my goodness. I haven't seen you in almost three years. You still got that body."

Swirvae blushing,

"Why, thank you, Kory. You don't look bad yourself."

Sometimes, I find myself daydreaming about Swirvae. The weekend we spent together will always be a lasting memory. People ask me why my smile is so bright. I don't answer. But I'm still smiling. You short, sexy, sassy woman. Seems like all the women in my life are under 5'3.

Swirvae hugged me again.

"Kory, I think about you all the time. Nobody ever made me feel the way you do. You kiss me like you love me. Thank you so much."

Swirvae kissed me like she was in love all over again. Something came up.

"Oh yeah, this is my cousin, Wayne."

Wayne is smiling really big. Now, he's laughing.

"So, you are the infamous Swirvae. I finally got to meet you. Everything Kory said about you is true. But I want to know one thing, Swirvae."

Swirvae is blushing.

"And what might that be, Mr. Wayne?"

Wayne is now standing with both hands in his pockets.

"Do you have a twin sister?"

We all laughed.

"No, Wayne. I don't have a twin sister."

Wayne looking disappointed.

"Well, damn, Swirvae. I thought we could do a double date. I guess not."

"No, Wayne, sorry." But I might have a friend I could hook you up with. I will have to get back with you later, Wayne."

Wayne is grinning and licking his lips.

"Sounds like a winner, Swirvae."

"Wayne and Swirvae, I hate to interrupt this loving moment but let us remember why we are here. My infidelity is one of the reasons I landed in rehab. I came here to clean up. Changing my life is all that's on my mind. It's important that I maintain the right state of mind. My wife and kids need me to stand up and be accountable. A new me must emerge from this center, totally rehabilitated."

We were in rehab for about 6 days.

"Wayne, I can't wait to see my wife."

"How soon before they get here, Kory?"

"Man, I just talked to Kara. They are about twenty minutes away from here."

"Kory, I am packed and ready to go."

* * * * *

Leaving Rehab

"Mama, is Daddy coming home today? I miss Daddy, mama."

"I miss Daddy, too, Kelsi. Ok, girls, get in the car. You and Alisha are staying with grandmama while I go get Daddy."

"Mama, are you driving all the way to Houston by yourself?"

"No, Alisha. Toni is going with me."

"Oh, ok mama."

"Ok, girls, tell mama I will be back tomorrow. Be good and don't watch TV all night. Give me a hug, Kelsi."

"Humm uh. Bye, mama."

"Bye, Kelsi."

"Alisha, are you too big to give your mama a hug?"

"No mama. Humm-uh. Bye, mama. Drive safe. See you tomorrow."

"Ok, bye babies."

I need to call Toni right quick.

"Hello."

"Toni, it's Kara. I'm on the way to your house. I'll be there in 5 minutes."

"Ok, Kara. I'm walking down the steps now. I see you coming. Pop the trunk so I can put my suitcase in. Hey, Kara."

"Hey Toni. Look at you all dressed up and wearing stilettos. Wayne will be trying to get some in the back seat."

"Girl, you are so right. We might have to get a room before we get back home. I just got off the phone with him. He said he is about to bust."

Toni and I laughed.

"Same here, girl. I think Kory has made reservations at some hotel for the night. I got a suitcase, too."

Toni and I talked as we traveled Interstate 45 to Houston. The old-school music was blasting on the radio.

"Toni, I prayed last night. It's been a while since I last prayed. I want my marriage with Kory to work. For this marriage to work, two people need to change. Kory is taking the right steps to change. On my knees,

I asked the Lord to change me. This is the only way it will work."

"My Daddy used to say, "*Change is inevitable.*"

He was a bitter man for a long time. His anger made him hard to live with. The other day I was at my mom's house and the phone rang. Mama started to cry and dropped the phone. I picked up the phone from the floor and answered it. Angry, I asked, 'who the hell is this making my mama cry?' He answered,

"Kara, this is Daddy. How are you doing, baby?" I started crying.

"Daddy, is it really you? Where are you? I didn't think I would ever hear from you again."

He replied,

"Yeah, it's me, Kara. I live in Beaumont, Texas now. For many years, I traveled the country. Now, I am ready to come home to my family. Can I come back home, Kara?"

Crying, I answered.

"Yes, Daddy, you can come back home. I miss you, Daddy."

Mama grabbed the phone and told me to go home.

"Toni, I don't know what happened when I left mama's house. When I get back home, I will wait a couple of days before I talk to her about Daddy."

"Kara, I would love to be a fly on the wall and hear the conversation between your mom and dad."

"You and me both, Toni."

"So, what was your reaction when your mom told you to go home, Kara?"

"Toni, I got my purse, told the girls to get in the car and went home."

Toni laughed and wiped her tears. Seeing her laugh made me laugh.

"What's so funny Toni?"

"Kara, I have never seen your mother get mad. She is a quiet, easygoing woman. I wish I could have seen the look on your face."

Toni is laughing, holding her side.

"Well, anyway, I hope they can work things out, Toni. My daughters ask me about my Daddy all the time. Maybe, they will finally get to meet him. It will be nice to put the family back together again.

"Well, maybe so, Kara. That would be nice. I hope things work out for you."

"Thanks, Toni."

Houston, Texas, we finally made it. Kory and Wayne loaded their bags in the car. Kory insisted on driving.

"Kory, slow down. If you don't get a ticket, we will all end up dead."

Kory is excited and driving with one hand on the steering wheel. His right hand is caressing my legs uncontrollably. With a horny look on his face, he replied.

"Sorry, Kara. There's a Residence Inn not far from here. I think it's on Interstate 45. Ok, there it is. I will go inside of the office with Wayne and get the room keys. Kara, you and Toni find a parking space."

"Toni, girl, this is too funny. Our guys are running around like chickens with their heads cut off."

Toni and I parked the car and had a good laugh.

"Kara, I think if I ask Wayne for a new house right now he would say yes without question."

I gave Toni a high five.

"Toni, be sure to get all new furniture, too."

We laughed with tears in ours eyes. Looking through the rearview mirror, I see Kory waving his hands trying to get my attention.

"Hey, are you two coming? Let's go, Kara. We got the rooms."

"Toni, girl, let's get the luggage and go. I can already see how this will end." Kory is giving Wayne some dap.

"Wayne, we will talk with you and Toni later."

I tried not to laugh at my husband.

"Kory, slow down, baby. I know it's been a while. I'm wearing high heels. I bought this dress just for you Kory. Do you like it?"

Kory is looking for the room number. He is not paying me any attention.

"Yeah, yeah, yeah, Kara. It looks good. I always have trouble with these room keys. The light is not coming on."

"Let me try, Kory. Ok, we're in. Kory, this room is cold. Check the thermostat, please?"

Kory walked to the other side of the room to check the thermostat.

"The thermostat is fine.   Come on, Kara.   Get undressed."

"I have to use the bathroom first, Kory.   Get that frustrated look off your face."

"Ok Kara, hurry up."

"What are you doing, Kory? Close the bathroom door, Kory."

"Hurry up, Kara. I need to pee, too. I'm waiting on you. What's so funny, Kara?"

"You are so funny, Kory. Ok, I'm done, Kory."

"Ooh Kara, you feel so good. We might not make it to the bed."

"Don't stop hugging me, Kory. I like this. You should go to rehab more often if this is what it feels like when you come home."

"My beautiful wife. Damn, you fine. I missed you so much, Kara. Lay down on the bed baby. Did you bring the music?"

"It's on my cell phone, Kory. Let me turn on some slow, love-making music. Kory, you are breathing hard. Slow down. Make it last. Slow down, Kory."

"Kara, Kara. Ohhhh yes. Ohhhh yes. Yessss."

Silence.

"Well darn, Kory. I know you're not sleep. Wake up, Kory. Kory, wake up. You're snoring in my ear. That wasn't even a whole minute. Get off me… You are too funny, Kory. But I love you."

* * * * *

Changing Lives

Early the next morning, we drove back to Tyler. Kory is half sleep.

"Kory, what was rehab like?" Taking a deep breath, he explained.

"Well, baby, rehab was an eye-opening experience. I had already read the 12 steps book. So, I was already familiar with the information. Rehab gave me a chance to take a good look at myself. I have made a lot of mistakes. I am truly sorry for all the problems I caused in our marriage. I hope you can forgive me."

Tears begin to flow down my face.

"I didn't mean to make you cry, baby."

"Kory, this is the very first time you have ever apologized to me about anything. You sound sincere, hallelujah. How do we keep this going, Kory?"

"Applying the knowledge learned in rehab is essential to growth, Kara. We must get involved in community activities and go to the meetings."

"What kind of meetings, Kory?"

"The meetings are kind of like AA meetings except they call them CA meetings. I think CA stands for cocaine anonymous. Wayne and I are supposed to report to the meeting on Monday or as soon as possible."

Looking in the rearview mirror, I spoke to Wayne.

"Wayne, are you and Kory going to be alright?"

"Kara, the two of us are going to be the best men you have ever seen. You and Toni will be pleased. The counselor said recovery is a long, slow process. Stay away from things that tempt you to use drugs. Keep away from old hangouts and old friends. Recovery is about a lifestyle change."

"Wayne, that sounds good. Looks like the two of you have the information to get it right. Stay with it."

Wayne looked at me and shook his head ok.

"Kara, leave Wayne alone."

"Kory, I don't mean any harm. The two of you do everything together. Not only are you cousins but you are best friends. It is important that the two of you focus on the same goal. I want the both of you to win. That is all I am saying, Kory. Besides he's my cousin too. Are you my cousin, Wayne?"

Everyone chuckled.

"Yeah, Kara. I'm your cousin, too. I feel you, Kara."

Toni touched Kory on his shoulder and Wayne on his knee.

"Wayne and Kory, Kara and I just want the two of you to win. That's all Kara is saying."

Toni whispers in Wayne's ear.

"Wayne, I want to win with you. I have my own apartment now. Here is your key."

"I see the two of you in my rearview mirror, kiss, kiss, kiss."

Kory is looking at me.

"Kara, stop being nosy. We have some kissing of our own to do. Keep your eyes on the road. Get home as quick as you can."

The wrinkle in the middle of Kory's forehead made me laugh.

"I'm not laughing at you, Kory. But I'm guessing you are feeling another sudden burst of energy."

I see Wayne in my rearview mirror. He looked at me over the top of his glasses.

"Kory, Kara's got jokes?"

We laughed and enjoyed each other's company all the way home. It was a good trip. We arrived at the Cascades Apartments to drop off Toni. Wayne got out of the car with Toni. Kory is talking to Wayne.

"Hey man, where are you going?"

Wayne smiled as he and Toni hugged.

"Well, Kory, it looks like my life is changing. It is time for me to stop playing and get serious."

Looking up toward heaven Wayne said,

"Thank you. Today is a new day. We will holla at you and Kara later, kinfolk."

Kory and Wayne shook hands. Toni and Wayne went in their apartment. Kory and I picked up the girls and went home.

* * * * *

Mr. Preacher

Monday after work, Wayne and I went to our first CA meeting. We parked our vehicles across the street. We stood there for a moment and talked about our lives. We were not in a hurry.

"Wayne, check out the name on the building, 'The Meeting Hub'."

Wayne laughed.

"Yeah, Kory, I have been here before. There is always something going on here. They throw some good parties here, man."

"Well, this is my first time here, Wayne. If these group meetings are anything like rehab, there will be a lot of screaming and crying."

"Kory, man, I just want to get this chapter of my life behind me. Come on, let's cross the street and go inside."

"Do you smell that bread, Wayne?"

"Yeah, I do. It reminds me of when we were Cub Scouts. We made a field trip to Rose Family Bakery. They served us bread that was hot out of the oven. It wasn't sliced. Man, that bread was good. They put butter and honey on it and gave us chocolate milk."

"Dang, Wayne. You still remember that? We were in elementary. Father Epps and Ms. Warren used to take care of us. He was a good man."

"Kory, just standing here on Erwin Street brings back a lot of memories. Where did the time go?"

"I tell you where the time went, Wayne. We were too busy living somebody else's life. This Baller lifestyle isn't quite working out. The both of us have made some bad choices. Those bad choices have sent our lives in a whirlwind. Death has looked us in the face on more than one occasion. We have got to make this work."

"You said a mouthful, Kory. It will be good to hear how other people handle problems like ours."

Walking inside of the building, we stopped in the lobby. An older gentleman was sitting on top of a desk waiting to greet us.

"Are you guys here for the meeting?"

We both answered at the same time.

"Yes, sir, we are here for the meeting."

The older gentleman looked at me, and I looked at him.

"Hey, young man, don't I know you?"

I replied.

"Yes, sir. How are you doing, Mr. Preacher? My truck was impounded by your tow service. We met when I picked it up."

Smiling and shaking his head he replied.

"I remember now. You're Stump's nephew."

"Yes sir. My name is Kory. This is my cousin, Wayne. He is my uncle's son."

The gentleman looked at Wayne.

"Yeah, you got that Evander Holyfield build like your Daddy. You got that big head too, son."

The three of us laughed.

"You fellas, write your name on the sign-in sheet. Now, follow me to the photo room. One at a time, I want you to stand on the 'X' and look at the camera. When your picture comes up on the computer screen, step over to the keyboard on the table. I want you to write a couple of sentences about yourself. We do things a little different here. The reason for this information is to keep track of your progress. You can log into the website from home and update your weekly information."

As Wayne and I logged off the computer, a woman walked up behind me. She put her hands around my head and covered my eyes. With her breast pressed against my back she spoke,

"Guess who?" Her perfume filled the air. I turned around slowly and made eye contact with the woman that I most wanted to forget. She's smiling from ear to ear. Speaking in a high-pitched, baby voice,

"It's me, Amber! Do you remember me from The Party Shack?"

She hugged me tight like we were old friends. I grabbed her arms and moved her away from me.

"You are still crazy. Where is your girlfriend who tried to cut my arm off?"

She held her head down like she was embarrassed.

"I am not with her anymore. I'm sorry for what happened to you. Do you forgive me?"

Wayne is standing behind her, shaking his head in disbelief.

Mr. Preacher spoke, "The meeting is getting ready to start."

I answered, "Yes, sir."

We walk out of the sign-in room to find a seat. Wayne looks like he trying to hide from someone.

"Kory, let's sit in the back. Some of these crackheads might recognize us."

"You're right, Wayne. There are some familiar faces in this place. Most of them are trying to hide, too."

"Why are they trying to hide, Kory? They must owe you money?"

"You said it, Wayne. I'm thinking about taking my hat off and holding it in my hand like a collection plate."

"Don't waste your time, Kory. Remember we are all here for the same reason. To tell the truth, I am a bit reluctant to share my mistakes in life with people from my community. It's not like being in Houston with people who don't know me. People in Tyler are nosy as hell."

"You can say that again, Wayne. But it's not about them. This is about fixing our lives."

"This meeting will come to order."

After Mr. Preacher call the meeting to order, we went through everything we did in rehab. Finally, he recognized me and Wayne.

"You two guys state your name and tell us about yourselves."

"My name is Kory, and I'm a substance abuser and a Baller wannabe."

The group responded.

"Hi, Kory."

Then Wayne introduced himself.

"My name is Wayne, and I am a substance abuser and a Baller wannabe."

"Hi, Wayne."

Somebody is laughing loud.

"Mr. Preacher, why are they substance abusers and the rest of us are crackheads?"

Everyone in the room laughed. Damn, I was so embarrassed. Wayne and I took a closer look at this person. It was none other than Slim janky.

Mr. Preacher spoke again.

"Well, now we have all formerly met. Are there any questions?"

There was silence.

"Remember, you can ask anything and talk about anything in these meetings. Nothing is off limits."

My cousin spoke up.

"Mr. Preacher, I have a question."

Mr. Preacher was glad that someone had a question.

"What's your question, Wayne?"

"Well, sir, looking around this room all I see are African-American males and females. Did God really curse us in the Bible? The world hates us. They tell us to forget about slavery. Well, I did some research on the treatment of slaves. There is no way I will ever forget it. We medicate to ease the pain. When we come down from our high, nothing has changed. Nowadays, the courts are filling up prisons with black males. If they don't put you in prison, the police kill you. Seldom are they prosecuted. When does it end? Will God ever forgive us?"

Tears ran down Wayne's face.

"Are we descendants of Ham?"

I put my arm around Wayne. Mr. Preacher walked from the front of the room to the back where me and Wayne were sitting. He told Wayne,

"Stand up, Wayne."

Wayne stood up, and Mr. Preacher hugged Wayne like he was his own son. Tears were flowing throughout the room. After he stopped hugging Wayne, Mr. Preacher walked back to the front of the room.

"Wayne, the answer to your question is no. We are not descendants of Ham. As a matter of fact, the story of Noah and the Ark was made up. A lot of the stories in the Bible were taken from mythology, fables, allegory, and tales. A lot of the information comes from ancient Egyptian literature. I have a lot of books on the bookshelf in back of the room that will show you where the stories of the Bible come from. The Bible teaches you faith, but the stories are not necessarily true. When you think about something being true, consider the source of the information. I have a video by Dr. John Henrik Clark that can explain this better. But think about this everyone. Most religions are written at the end of a war. The loser gets plundered."

Slim Janky interrupted,

"What's plundered, Mr. Preacher?"

"That means the winner of the war takes the loser's possessions. The winner becomes the oppressor, and the loser becomes the oppressed. The winner kills, steals, and rapes the oppressed. The winner also changes the bloodline and culture of the loser. Documents are then written to control the people who the oppressor does not kill. The best way to control people is to take religious documents they are familiar with and change the documents. People don't ask questions when it comes to religion. They believe everything in the Bible. Think about it. How many times have you or your parents questioned the Bible? Never. But at the end of a war, the winner will write a set of rules or concessions for the loser to live by. If you break the rules, you die. The rules are not necessarily God's word. Over 2000 years, we have been living according to the rules written by the Romans. The Romans were evil people. They won the war against Hannibal. The Romans heavily taxed and oppressed the Egyptians. The Egyptians questioned if God would save them. Then, the Romans wrote a new religion for the Egyptians to live by. The religion was written to control the Egyptians. The religion is now known as European Christianity and the new testament. I kind of got off the subject, but I want you to know where religions come from. Religions do not come from God. Man writes religions. Man writes religions, but man does not use the religion he writes. If you go to a Catholic Church, you will find out they seldom read from the King James Bible. They wrote it, but they don't use it."

"Let me tell you all one more thing, and then you can go."

Historians, scholars and Egyptologists of all races have searched the world for the origin of their religion. They all end up in the same place, the Nile valley in Africa. Some of the historians were Gerald Massey, A.H.L. Heeren, Court Volney and Sir E.A. Wallis Budge. The truth about the Bible has been known for many years. The problem has been reporting the truth. The origins of Christianity have been openly denied or secretly suppressed. Bringing new researched information back to the United States in the 1700 and 1800 would get a researcher blackballed. The researcher could not receive scholarship money for future expeditions. They would put the information in storage and wait until the time was right to present the information. Some researchers would go as far as to write books of propaganda. Propaganda material is written to deliberately throw the reader off the path of the truth."

"In today's world if you say anything contrary to the Bible people get very upset. So, when you learn the information that I am about to give you, be careful. Never say anything bad about another person's religion.

People have the right to believe anything they want to. Use research information to build confidence in yourself. Use the information to discover your gift. Once you discover your gift, your gift must be developed. Use your gift to become the best person you can be. Find happiness and prosperity. Then, you will be in Heaven.

"Also, some notable Black historians are Yosef Ben Jochannan, John G. Jackson, John Henrik Clark, Chancellor Williams, Cheikh Anta Diop and many more. They, along with others, went back to Africa and lived for a while. They researched, lectured and wrote books. Their lectures are on video. Go on YouTube and watch Dr. Clark's 'Jews and Africans Relationship.' This video will explain the truth behind the Exodus. Watch all the videos by the historians. The answer to your question about the curse of Hem is included, Wayne."

Amber interrupted.

"Mr. Preacher?"

He replied, "Yes, Amber."

"Mr. Preacher, I have heard the Exodus sermon before. They roamed the desert for 400 years. You know, my Daddy is a preacher."

The whole room erupted with laughter. Slim Janky could not help himself.

"Your Daddy is a preacher? The preacher has a crackhead daughter? Are you kidding?"

The laughter in the room is exceedingly loud.

Mr. Preacher responded.

"In Ambers defense, the devil comes to the preacher's house first."

I looked at Mr. Preacher with my eyebrows stretched upward. He laughed and held his side.

Mr. Preacher continued.

"That's about all the time we have for tonight."

Everyone stood up and started talking as they left the building.

"Take a book home with you and read it. I have a lot of books on the bookshelf."

"Mr. Preacher."

"Yes, Slim Janky."

"Do you want us to read this big, old book by next week? It will take me six months to read this big old thing."

"That book is 'The Africans Who Wrote the Bible' by Nana Darkwah. It's a good book. Take it home and read it, Slim Janky."

"Ok, there are plenty of other books to choose from. There are also videos of Dr. John Henrik Clark and Dr. Yosef Ben Jochannan. These men are historical researchers and Egyptologists. All the books are on my Facebook page. Go to my Facebook page and click on any book. You will be redirected to another page where you can buy the book. Please buy some of the books. Also, when I think of something that might help you, I will send you a message. Goodnight and drive safe. Let's close with a prayer."

"Kory, I need to talk to Slim Janky right quick."

"Ok, Wayne. I'm trying to avoid this crazy woman."

We walked across the room to talk to Slim Janky.

"Slim Janky, you remember the night we got stopped by the police? Where did that story about the ice cream come from? You sounded like you knew what you were talking about. Kory, you should have been there."

Wayne and I looked at Slim Janky waiting for an answer. He answered,

"Well, fellas, you know I have a college degree."

In disbelief, Wayne had to sit down.

"You got a college degree?"

Slim replied.

"I got a college degree in Air Conditioning and Refrigeration. Some people call me Shade Tree A/C. The two of you look surprised."

I responded.

"One thing I have learned not to do is judge people."

He shook his head in agreeance.

"Here is the thing Wayne and Kory. When you are dealing with police officers, you never know which kind you will get. Sometimes you get a good one, but here lately most of the time you get a hard-headed one. Use psychology to see what kind of guy he is. Most of the time, you can talk your way out of a situation. Have your driver's license, insurance and registration ready when he asks for it. If the police officer is a hard head, every time he asks you a question say *lawyer*. Don't say anything else except *lawyer*. More than anything…stay alive. Stay alive and help bring about change in society. You can't change anything if you are dead. I got to run, fellas. See you guys next time."

We all shook hands and walked away.

"Wayne, watch my back."

"What's up, Kory?"

"I recognize one of the guys in class from the shootout at The Gambling Shack. Check out the guy in the green shirt with half of one ear shot off."

Wayne turned slowly and looked at the guy.

"Yeah, kinfolk. I see him. You know I felt like somebody was watching me the whole time we were here. No worry. I got my gun in the truck. Let's get our books and go."

Mr. Preacher was walking back into his office.

"Kory and Wayne, let me talk to you before you go."

Wayne and I went into the office to see what Mr. Preacher wanted.

"Have a seat, fellas. Before the two of you go, I have some community service for you. As part of your rehabilitation, community service is required for one year. During this time, you will volunteer at a different location each month. I will email you the list of companies. Starting tomorrow, you will be volunteering at The Food Bank. You will also get a chance to work with a lot of kids. Don't take this lightly fellas. This will help you to be better men."

* * * * *

Angelle Calls

"We need to turn a couple of corners before we go home Wayne. I want to make sure this guy isn't following us."

Wayne nodded his head in agreement.

"For sho,' kinfolk. I got my eye on this guy. I will follow you in my car."

We got in our vehicles and proceeded to drive through random areas of town. I called Wayne on my cell phone.

"Wayne, let's drive by The Party Shack. I'm not stopping, just driving by."

"Ok, Kory, I'm close behind you."

"There is no sign of his car anywhere, Wayne. I'm going home."

"Yeah, me too, Kory. I don't see any signs of this guy. See you at work tomorrow."

"Ok, Wayne, I will see you tomorrow.

Half way home my phone rang.

"Hello."

"Hi, Kory."

I hesitated before I answered,

"Hey, Angelle.

"Kory, I haven't heard from you in a while. Are you still mad? Do you ever think about me?"

"Yeah, I think about you, Angelle. But I have been too busy trying to get my life together. No, I am not mad, just disappointed how things turned out. You held back information that was critical in our relationship."

"I'm sorry, Kory. I should have told you everything. I was afraid you wouldn't want to be with me. Every night, I look at my wedding dress and cry myself to sleep. My heart aches. Come by my house as soon as you can, Kory. I have a present for you. Ok, Kory?"

"Angelle I am turning into my driveway. I have to go now."

"Ok, Kory. I still love you."

"Ok, Angelle. I'll see you…. Bye."

"Bye, Kory."

* * * * *

Stick Man

The next morning as I was getting ready for work, Kara got up and fixed breakfast.

"How was the meeting, Kory? Do you think it helped?"

We sat down at the dining room table.

"The meeting went well, Kara. I think it is a step in the right direction. This morning, I woke up without a hangover."

Kara choked on her coffee.

"Well, that's an improvement already, Kory."

"That's not funny, Kara. When I get off work, I'm supposed to report to community service. I don't know what time I will be home."

Kara kissed me goodbye.

"We will be here when you get home, Kory. Bye, love you."

"Love you, too, baby."

While at work, I got an email from Mr. Preacher. We were on our lunch break.

"Wayne, did you get an email from Mr. Preacher?"

"Yeah, Kory, I did. I read it, but it didn't make a lot of sense. He said something about a stick man."

I'll check it out after community service tonight.

When I got home, I logged into the CA website for the first time. I set up my password. There is an email flashing. When I opened the email, there was a paragraph welcoming me to the group. The instructions said print your picture and personal information that was entered at this week's meeting. After you print the information, hang it on the wall. Draw a stick man on a separate sheet of paper. Take the stick man and place it over your picture. Do not cover the information underneath the picture. Here is the question. Does placing the stick man above your personal information give him life? Does the stick man exist? Let me call Wayne.

"Hello."

"Wayne, did you read the email from Mr. Preacher?"

"Yeah, I read it. I don't know what the hell he is talking about."

"Same here, Wayne. But there is a second part to the email. 'I want you guys to report to the practice field behind the Legacy Building. The Legacy Building is located behind Rose Stadium. Go tomorrow after work and ask for Coach Jeff. The two of you will be working with kids in the football league. It's playoff time.'

The next day after work, we reported to the football field. Spending time with the kids really put things in perspective. This is much more important than using drugs and hanging out with thugs. It is a whole lot better than picking up trash on the side of the highway. The single moms don't look too bad either. A lot of these boys don't have a male figure present in their lives. It feels good to be a positive influence on a young boy's life.

"Kory, I haven't run this much since I was in high school. I'm a pretty good teacher. I got the defense on and popping. This is great! Coach Jeff said something about taking some classes to make things official. So, when I have a son, I can teach him how to play football. I'm loving this, Kory!"

"Yeah, I can see you are, Wayne. They need to put a football uniform on you."

We both laughed.

"Kory, don't forget we are not working tomorrow."

"We are not working? What are you talking about, Wayne?"

"They are doing inventory tomorrow, remember?"

"Oh, yeah that's right. I'll see you tomorrow at football practice, Wayne. Later."

"Ok, Kory, later."

* * * * *

Kory's Test

Friday morning, *beep, beep, beep, beep, beep, beep*. Turn off that alarm. *Beep, beep, beep, beep, beep, beep*. Cell phone reminder. Wedding day is coming. That's why Angelle called me the other night. She mentioned her wedding dress. Well, damn. I think I'll get dressed and go fishing to sort things out. My wife and kids are already gone.

I wonder if Kara made coffee before she went to work. *Ring, ring, ring,*

"Hello."

"Kory,"

"Hey, Uncle Jessie. How you doing?"

"Oh, son, I'm doing ok for an old man. I just called to remind you that the Brotherhood at our church is having a fellowship lunch in a couple of days. Why don't you cook some of that world-famous bar-b-que of yours? Everyone seems to like it. They say it's almost as good as mine, hahahahaha."

We both laugh. I replied,

"Ok, Unk, I sure will. I've had a taste for some ribs myself."

So off to the store I go. Walking across the parking lot of the grocery store, I'm reminded of what happened the last time I was here. A tow truck is removing somebody's car from the parking lot. This time, I will stay focused and remember why I am here. A courtesy clerk greeted me as soon as I walked in the door.

"How are you doing, sir? Come on in."

I replied,

"Oh, I'm doing pretty good. Thanks for asking."

"Are you looking for anything particular, sir? Everything in the meat section is on sale."

I replied,

"As a matter of fact, I am looking for some meat to bar-b-que. Thanks for the information."

He's still talking.

"If you need some help with something just let me know, sir. By the way, aren't you the guy who left his truck in the parking lot?"

He laughs and now I am embarrassed. I answered,

"You know, I heard about that. But no, it wasn't me. Thanks for asking."

We both laughed.

Walking through the store, I always see somebody I know.

"Hey, what's up, Kory?"

"Alright, what's going on, player?"

People know my name, but I don't know who the hell they are.

Arriving at the meat counter, I check out the briskets. Holding the brisket flat I bend it end to end. If the two ends meet, it means the brisket is tender and not full of fat. The ribs look fantastic too, thick and meaty. There is a pretty good selection of chicken wings, shrimp, hot dogs and Earl Campbell links. It's about to be on. The store is full of women. Maybe, I should come here instead of going to the night club.

Oh yeah, I need some seasoning. Let me see if they have some Lips Smackers Seasoning Salt. Lips Smackers has good sauce, too. Walking up the spice aisle looks like they are sold out. Darn.

Somebody called me a name that I haven't heard in two years.

"Big Dog, what up?"

An infamous voice shouted out. Trying to ignore the person, I responded under my breath,

"Gottt…dang it."

He heard what I said,

"Naw…good dope. It's G.D. I know you remember me the way we used to hang. Man, where you been in the joint, out of town…what?"

We shook hands like homies do. I replied,

"Well, I've been trying to get back. A lot of things have changed in my life. I was forced to make a decision about my future. When you are faced with an epiphany, you learn how to make good decisions. Some of us can't change without ultimatums. The life that I once lived had to end. All negativity in my life had to cease. Surrounding myself with people who have the same goals in life that I do seems to be working for me. Positive people and a positive environment are shaping me into the man I always knew I could be."

G.D. looked at me over the top of his sunglasses and responded,

"Already."

I said,

"Already."

Right about then another guy walked up and joined our conversation. G.D. introduced him,

"Big Dog, this my nephew. I call him Thang-Thang because he be selling them thangs, hahahahaha."

His nephew spoke,

"Alright, Big Dog. I saw you at the city impound when you came to get your truck."

I looked at G.D.'s nephew and said,

"Yeah, yeah, now I remember. You are the guy with the dog. It's been a minute."

Thang-Thang extended his hand to shake my hand, and I felt him place something in between my fingers all the way to the soft tissue. It's a gigantic rock that made my fingers go numb. Not wanting to look, I opened my hand and took a sneak peek. The color is goldish brown, and the smell is so strong it's making me high right here in the store. It's that butta.

I immediately closed my eyes and asked the Lord for strength against temptation. I pray a good prayer and when I open my eyes G.D. and his nephew are staring at me. They look at me like something is growing out of my skull and about to take flight. I guess they haven't prayed in a while. If I speak in tongues, they might freak out and run. My confidence level is high as I speak to G.D.

"Man, this is not the life that I live anymore. I'm a better man now, and on top of that, I can't afford it."

G.D. is like,

"Player, you know the two of us are cool. We used to hang hours at a time. Tell you what. Take it for old time's sake. You don't owe me nothing. Me and you dawgz, player."

Thang-Thang had stepped back and let me and G.D. talk. I looked at the rock again and something in my mind said,

"Yeahhhh,"

But I couldn't do it. I thought about the many nights I cried...sweated until the bed was soaking wet...had nightmares...lonely nights and finally getting on my knees and praying to God. There is no way I can ever go back to that life again. The devil is a lie. G.D. started to walk away and I put the rock in his front shirt pocket.

"I'm done, G.D. I'm done."

Rolling my grocery cart away, I keep praying because I know when I turn at the end of the aisle, he will be standing there. I keep praying, 'Lord I can't do this on my own. Fix it Lord.' When I got to the next aisle, I didn't see him. Walking from aisle to aisle, my spirit began to get excited. The two of them were nowhere to be found. I walked around the whole store and didn't see them anywhere. They vanished into thin air. That was my test. I shouted to the top of my voice,

"Thank You!! ... Thank You!! ... Thank You!"

Somebody a couple of aisles over echoed,

"Tell Him 'thank you'!"

And the sound of a tambourine fills the store, *tacky toom, tacky toom, tacky toom, tacky toom.*

Finally, my Aunt Jackie grabbed me,

"Come here, baby."

I didn't even know she was in the same store. She hugged me, and I calmed down. Aunt Jackie said,

"I saw you when you came in the store. Then, I watched those thugs approach you. I'm proud of my nephew. That's how you handle life's temptations. Call on God. Stay prayed up, and he will never leave you."

We left the store together. The spirit of the Lord has put me in an emotional state that I have never experienced.

* * * * *

Driving Home

Driving home, a car passed me playing music so loud I couldn't hear the music playing in my truck. When I stopped at the red light, the music seemed to get even louder. This familiar music is bringing back memories of times that I have really been trying to forget. Here lately, I have been listening to a lot of gospel music. But for a moment, my life flashed back to my night clubbing days. Smoke in the air...the music is bumping...and a drink in my hand. Maybe I'll drive over to the Super Corner and holla at the fellas...Maybe not? The rock that Thang-Thang put between my fingers has me all messed up. This must be another test. That's it! Everything that I have learned over the last two years tells me this is a test. It's a test of my faith in God. There will always be a test, but making the right decision is gold. I need to hear some James Cleveland, lol. Somebody told me that the music you listen to influences the person that you will eventually become. Positive thoughts, positive people and positive environment help to build a positive spirit and a positive life. I've come too far to blow it now. But negative thoughts are haunting me. Going home sounds like a better idea.

Being home feels good. It's my safe haven. I think I'll season the meat and marinate it for tomorrow's

Brotherhood lunch at church. Shake some of this and shake some of that. This will be some of the best bar-b-que they ever had. My phone is beeping, and it's a message from Uncle Jessie. I answered,

"Hello, Uncle Jessie."

He replied,

"Son, my wife told me what happened at the grocery store, and I am so proud of you. But you need to prepare yourself. Prepare yourself for the fight of your life. The devil wants you back and tonight will be challenging to say the least. He will come strong and hard so stay prayed up to resist the temptation."

I replied,

"Ok, Unk. I will, thanks."

Preparing the bar-b-que seemed to take my mind off things. Now the bar-b-que is ready, and I am sampling some of these delicious, juicy ribs. I think I'll check out one of these old boxing matches while I'm sitting here in front of the TV. This shrimp and Earl Campbell hot links taste good, too. I'll finish this cold beer and chill in my recliner for a minute.

* * * * *

Bad News

"Kory, wake up. I picked up the girls from gymnastics. While sitting inside of the waiting area, a guy from The Party Shack recognized me. It was Big Tilly's little brother, Wolf. One of his ears looked like it had been shot off. I thought they all died that night at The Party Shack. He walked by me and called me *Ms. Ma'am*. I turned and looked over my shoulder as he walked by me."

I could feel the wrinkles in my forehead.

"Kara, why was he there?"

"Kory, as we were leaving, I saw him talking to the gymnastics teacher. He may be dating her. I don't know."

Shaking my head in disgust,

"Damn, Kara, I thought that chapter of our lives was over. Here we go again. If one of those guys is alive, we cannot rest. Don't worry, I will take care of it."

"Check your purse. Your cell phone is ringing, Kara."

"Hello. Hi, mama."

"Kara, come over here.   Bring Kory and the kids. Come now."

"Mama, what's the matter?   Mama sounds excited, Kory."

"I will tell you when you get here."

"Ok, mama we are on the way.   Girls get back in the car. We are going to grandmother's house. Kory let's go check on mama."

"Ok, Kara. It sounds like something is wrong."

I grabbed two of my double-barreled pistols on the way out of the house.

"I will get to Ms. Murphy's house as soon as I can, Kara."

These narrow country roads are not made for the speed that I am traveling.

"Kory, drive around the loop to North Broadway. That will take you straight to 24th street."

"Kara, I know the way to your mother's house.   Sit back and relax. Everybody put your seatbelts on. Hold on. Here we go."

"Daddy, you are driving really fast. Daddy, you are scaring me. You almost hit one of the deer that was crossing the road."

"Ok, Alisha. Daddy will slow down. I don't want to scare my babies."

My babies were smiling.

"Thank you, Daddy. I hope grandma is ok."

Kara turned around and talked to the girls as they looked out of the back window. We made it to North Tyler in a matter of minutes. If Big Tilley's little brother is in the house, he is a dead man.

I parked the car as quickly as possible.

"Kara, y'all stay in the car."

The next thing I know, Kara was on my heels. The girls were close behind her. We all ran to the front door. Mrs. Murphy opened the door, and Kara screamed. I pushed Kara and the girls to the side of the door. With a gun in both hands, I entered the house with arms spread wide. Somebody is about to get blasted.

Kara screamed at the top of her voice.

"Nooo, Kory! That's my Daddy, brother, sisters, nieces and nephews."

Everyone is on the floor hiding behind furniture. Standing in the middle of the room, I turned side to side waving my guns.

"Awww, hell. My bad. I guess I am a little overprotective these days. I'm sorry for scaring everyone."

Kara grabbed me from behind.

"Put the guns down, Kory." Everyone laughed and got up off the floor.

"Remind me not to break in your house, Kory."

Mr. Murphy laughed and hugged me.

"Hey, Mr. Murphy. How are you doing, sir?"

He laughed and replied.

"Besides wetting my pants, I think I'm ok. Those are Gilboa double barrel pistols. A friend of mine has some just like those."

Everyone is coming over to greet us. Kara can't control her crying. Emotions are running high.

"Kory, what's up, man? It's been a long time."

Looking at Don, Jr., we shake hands and hug. I responded,

"DJ, it has been a long time. How in the world are you doing?"

The look on his face was somewhere between a smile and a cry.

"Kory, I can't complain. It wouldn't do any good."

We laughed as Kara's sisters jumped in my arms.

"Pinky and Christina. How are the two of you doing?"

Looking me in the eye, they both laugh. Pinky replied,

"Well, I'm kind of sore from jumping over the sofa. I don't normally do that every day."

Christina also had remarks.

"Yeah, Kory, I always wanted to be in Wrestle Mania."

They are really laying it on thick. But it was all in fun. The kids were all laughing and glad to see each other. It has been a long time since we were all together. There is nothing like family.

"Listen, everyone. Why don't you all come to our house tomorrow for fun and food? Kory loves to cook on the grill. Maybe, he will let us shoot some of his guns."

DJ responded,

"That's a great idea. I would love to shoot some of Kory's guns. I bet you have a lot of nice guns, Kory."

I looked around the room and smiled in agreement.

"You could say I have a couple of firearms. I will set up some targets, and we will have a contest. How about that?"

Everyone agreed.

"Well, we had better go put the girls in bed. We will see you all tomorrow. Bye, everyone.

Let's go, Kory."

* * * * *

Kory is Shocked

The next day Kara's family came to our house for Christmas dinner. Kara and I prepared a feast. The family ate and got to know each other all over again. Kara was very emotional.

"I could not have asked for a better Christmas. I haven't seen my brother and sisters in a very long time. I think about you all every day. Everyone is smiling. I think we are going to be ok. Let's please keep in contact."

Everyone agreed.

"Mom."

"Yes, Alisha."

"I cannot believe you bought us bicycles."

"That was your dad's doing. He's the bicycle king."

Don, Jr., responded.

"Yeah, Alisha. Your dad can ride on one wheel. Kory to the rescue."

Everyone laughed and went outside.

The contest was next. We entered the woods behind my house, and the games began. I thought it would only be the guys shooting. Boy, was I wrong.

I set up targets on trees throughout the woods. This is going to be a fun event. Mr. Murphy was impressed by my collection of different weapons.

"Kory, these are some of the most interesting weapons I have ever seen."

Before he could insert the magazine in the gun, Kara grabbed a gun and started shooting. DJ congratulated her.

"Kara, good shot. You hit all the targets in the center. That's a perfect score."

After Kara finished shooting, she turned and looked at me. She didn't like the look on my face.

"What's the matter, Kory?"

She walked closer and hugged me.

"Kory, you have a look of confusion on your face. You have never seen me shoot a gun before."

Her dad noticed the look on my face, too. He walked over to me.

"Kory, I'm sure Kara told you about her childhood. After I returned home from work, the kids told me about the abusive housekeeper. I decided to teach my kids how to protect themselves. What happened to them was partly my fault. My wife's parents stole her from me. I was mad, sad and depressed. I took it hard. I am over it now. My kids are back in my life."

Kara kept hugging me.

"Mr. Murphy, what ever happened to the housekeeper?"

Mr. Murphy hesitated to answer.

"Well Kory, it's like this. Whenever you have some mess to clean up, you do it by yourself. Do not tell anybody about it. Twenty years later, do not tell anybody about it. You and Kara need to talk. I need to spend some time with my son."

He walked in the woods with DJ. Kara is reluctant to talk.

"We have been putting this conversation off far too long, Kara."

"Kory, can we please wait until everyone leaves? I just want to spend time with my dad and my siblings right now. I will tell you everything you want to know. I promise."

* * * * *

Kara's Confession

After everyone left, Kara and I did not speak to each other for a while. I sat at the dining room table. Kara walked by and glanced over at me a couple of times but said nothing. The girls are in their rooms. Kelsi comes out of her room.

"Daddy my game stopped working."

"The batteries are probably dead, Kelsi. I will get some batteries from my tool box and replace the old ones."

She smiles.

"Ok, Daddy."

Kara calls me,

"Kory, will you come in the bedroom, please?"

I close the door behind me. I sit on the bed and wait for Kara to speak. She is pacing the floor, smoking a cigarette. She walks over to the closet and pulls out a bottle of Hennessy. I never knew it was there. She removes the cork and drinks straight from the bottle. She's getting ready to lie. She takes a deep breath and so do I.

"Well, let's hear it, Kara."

She is stalling.

"What do you want to know, Kory?"

I fold my arms and give Kara my undivided attention.

"Start at the beginning, Kara. Why do people call you Ms. Ma'am? I don't get it. Where did you get that name?"

Standing directly in front of me, Kara begins to explain.

"Kory, it all started when you were staying out all night. When you came home I asked you where you had been and who were you with? You became violent and hit me for asking you where you had been until twelve o'clock the next day. I made my mind up to play the same game you were playing. Guys have been flirting with me since we were in high school. Your friends, Kory. I just never told you."

"Hold up, Kara. Guys have been flirting with you since we were in high school, and you never told me?"

She's raising her voice.

"That's right, Kory. I never told you."

I looked at Kara in disgust.

"Well, I guess you must have liked it, Kara. How is it possible for me to stop something if I don't know it is going on, Kara?"

Her neck is working side to side.

"Well, you should have known, Kory."

"So, what does that say about you, Kara? You are untrustworthy, and you like attention from other men. It sounds like I don't know my wife like I thought I did. You've got secrets, Kara. And you are blaming me for your bad choices in life. You know, it is funny, Kara. When I make mistakes, I get blamed for them. Also, when you make mistakes, I get blamed for your mistakes. At what point do you take responsibility for your own actions?"

Kara started to cry and spoke in a loud voice.

"Kory, it's not my fault."

"Childhood molestation changed my life. When I was a little girl, I was molested many times. I always have sexual thoughts. When I want to make love and you push me away, it makes me furious. Sometimes, I wonder if I am good enough. Those are the times when I think about killing myself."

With a surprised look on my face.

"Killing yourself, Kara?"

"Oh, now you are concerned, huh, Kory? Yes, I have thought many times of killing myself. I don't know what to do, Kory."

"Stop crying, Kara. Come here."

Kara sat on my knee. I hold her as she cries her heart out.

Now, I feel bad for calling her out. But we need to get it all out.

"Kara, stop crying and explain why people call you Ms. Ma'am."

She stopped crying and held her head down.

"Kory, the girls work for me. When I go out of town, Toni, Bambi, Melanin and Crush go with me. I make the deals with the guys, and the girls have sex with them. I collect the money and pay the girls as well."

I put both of my hands on my head and closed my eyes.

"Kara, I don't believe what I just heard. My wife and mother of my children is a pimp. I just be damned. Ain't this some shit. All this time, you said you were working for your job. But you were really pimping. I am the biggest damn fool in Texas."

Kara stood up and leaned against the dresser. She is starting to talk louder.

"Kory, I'm sorry. I never meant to hurt you. But I did not feel loved. Nobody ever loved me. You pushed me away too many times. What was I supposed to do? What about my life, Kory?"

Now, I am pissed.

"Kara, did you have sex with any guys?"

Kara flinched and stood up straight when I asked the question.

"Kara, did you have sex with any guys?"

She runs toward the bedroom door, and I grab her.

"Damn it, answer me! Answer me, Kara! I will choke the shit out of you."

The bedroom door opens. Alicia and Kelsi are screaming.

"Daddy, noo! Daddy please don't hurt mama! Daddy, please! Daddy, let mama go, Daddy. Please, Daddy!"

My baby girls are trying to pull my hands from around Kara's neck. Alisha stopped for a moment and placed her small hand on my face. My 15-year-old daughter looked me in the eye and spoke in a calm, relaxed voice.

"Daddy, mama has demons… you have demons, too. But me and Kelsi love the both of you unconditionally. Please don't hurt mama."

My anger faded away. I released my grip from around Kara's neck. With a numb body, I walked through the house. I grabbed the keys to my truck and left as fast as I could.

* * * * *

Wayne Encourages Kory

Bang, bang, bang.

"Who the hell is that knocking on my door at two o'clock in the morning?

"It's me, Wayne. It's Kory."

I hear the dead bolt slide as the door opens.

"Kory, what's wrong, man? Come on in. Have a seat on the sofa, man. Are you all right?"

Looking at my face, Wayne knows something is wrong.

"No, I'm not all right. Me and Kara just had a blow up. She been lying got damn since we have been together. I don't even know who she is."

"Kory, let me get you a drink."

Toni comes out of the bedroom.

"Hey, Kory. Are you all right?"

I look at Toni.

"Hey, Toni. Yeah, I'm all right."

Wayne got a bottle of scotch and two glasses. He looks at Toni,

"You go on back to bed, baby. Me and Kory might be up a while."

He sat in the recliner and faced me.

"Talk to me, kinfolk."

He fills my glass a third of the way. I drink the first shot fast. I was too embarrassed to look Wayne in the eye. Staring at my glass, I spoke.

"Man, Kara is a pimp. She's been pimping the girls for who knows how long. All those trips she's been going on for her job was a damn lie."

Wayne looked at me and shook his head.

"Yeah, Kory, my girl confessed, too. I wanted to kill her, but I didn't. I know you are hurting inside. You and Kara have been together for a long time. You all have two beautiful girls. Right now, you are mad as hell. But you need to find a way to forgive her and make it work. Your girls need you, and I know you can't imagine some other guy raising your kids."

Wayne is pissing me off. That is not what I wanted to hear.

"Wayne, what you talking about?"

Wayne had a slight grin on his face.

"Kinfolk, I want you to win. I will always have your back. For now, take a moment and step back. Look at your life, and you will see that I am right. You need to stay here tonight. If you go out in the streets, something might jump off. You can stay in the guest bedroom."

We shook hands and hugged.

"Thanks, Wayne."

I closed the door and got in bed. There was nothing on television that I wanted to watch. I decided to google childhood sexual abuse. There is a topic here that fits Kara, long-term effects of childhood sexual abuse. This page has everything on it that Kara and I talked about. Reading this information gives me a better understanding of Kara's condition. Her problem seems to be more serious than I thought. Maybe, I will call her and apologize. She needs counseling. I need counseling, and so do my baby girls. I wonder if Kara googled this same information. Uncle Jessie said she was way ahead of me. The scotch is kicking in.

The Dream

Where did all this smoke come from? Where the hell am I?

"Big Dog, you smoking the pipe or staring out the window?"

As I look around the room, I see some of my crack-smoking associates. There is a mattress placed on the floor in the middle of the room. I walk over and sit on one end. I answered,

"Yeah, I'm smoking the pipe. Stop hogging the pipe, Slim Janky. You are getting it too hot. It's about to break. Give me the pipe."

It's dark in here, and everyone is reaching for the pipe. There is a candle burning on the coffee table next to the mattress. I can't see who is in here. It's almost like they are hiding. People's faces are blurry. Maybe I am already high. Some of these people owe me money. That's why they are treating me like I'm the police.

A voice from the dark end of the mattress spoke.

"You talking or hitting the pipe?"

I asked,

"What's your name, player? I haven't seen you here before."

He replied,

"It ain't none of your business what my name is. Are you my Daddy?"

So, I asked him,

"Have you ever met your Daddy? Hell, you might be my boy. What's your mama's name? I been with a few scalawags."

Everyone laughed except him. Slim Janky looked at the guy and said,

"Who knows this guy?"

Everyone shaking they head like they don't know him.

New guy stands up and reaches in his back pocket like he's about to do something. The fight jumped off, and he got his butt kicked. On top of that the House man tells new guy to get the fuck out. New guy responds,

"My name Rabbit. I bought a rock and you told me I could use your pipe to smoke it."

As Rabbit is leaving, he tries to pull one of the women out with him, but she wasn't having it. Rabbit knew this sexy woman would turn into a sex fiend once she got full of dope. He didn't want anybody to touch her, but she put up a fight and stayed.

After new guy was thrown out, I cuddled up to new girl and made sure she got plenty to smoke. The freak show was on. Naked bodies were all over the room making sexually-satisfying noises. I laid back and closed my eyes hoping this night never ends. New girl got on top of me. Her sexual motions make me glad I am a man. I opened my eyes, and she started laughing. She said,

"I thought that would spark a memory."

It was Swirvae. Oh, my goodness. Nobody has ever satisfied me like Swirvae. She was moving to the musical rhythm playing on the little radio sitting underneath the coffee table.

"Ohhh, yes,"

Is all I can say. If I could bottle this up and sell it … I'd be a rich man. I'm about to…and *pow, pow, pow* gun fire erupted outside the house. Bullets are hitting inside the house. *Pow, pow, pow*. Somebody's doing a drive-by. *Pow, pow, pow*. Everyone is screaming and running trying to get out of the way of gun fire. *Boom, boom, boom*. House man returning fire and it sounds like a full-fledged war. People are always trying to rob dope houses. A dope fiend won't get a job, but he can get a gun. I just lost my high. My sex drive is going south with the quickness. Why am I here? *Pow, pow, pow, boom, boom, boom.* The shooting has intensified. I can hear empty shell casings falling on the floor. The dust in the air smells like fireworks on the Fourth of July. My clothes are wet and sticky from low crawling across the floor. The room is dark, and all I can do is ask the Lord to save me one more time. 'Lord, I know you are tired of me, but I want one more chance to fix my life.'

The shooting stops, and I hear footsteps running through the house. Ohhh shit … The guy with the gun is coming in the back door. No, wait a minute. The people in the house are running out the back door and jumping the fence behind the house. They are running as fast and as far as they can. I'm running, too. I call out in a loud voice,

"Swirvae, let's go!"

But she doesn't answer. I go back in the house and search the room again. She's been shot. Her blood is on my clothes. I run to the bathroom to get first aid supplies. I grab a towel and search the medicine cabinet. Nothing is there but an empty bottle of Robitussin.

As I close the medicine cabinet, I recognize the room in the mirror is not the room in which I'm standing. The picture on the wall, the vanity and even the items on top of the vanity look familiar. *Pow, pow, pow, boom, boom, boom.* Shots fire again. I fall on the floor and take cover. The police are here, lights flashing, and shooting at the gunman outside. *Tat-tat-tat, tat-tat-tat, tat-tat-tat, pow, pow, pow, tat-tat-tat.* A fierce gun battle is taking place outside. When the bullets stop flying, I am lying on the floor. Looking up, I see someone in the mirror. Slowly getting up off the floor, I stand in front of the mirror in shock. The man in the mirror is staring in utter disbelief...It's me talking to myself. It looks like I'm having a meltdown. I have lost my damn mind.

* * * * *

Wake Up

"Kory, kinfolk, wake up. Are you alright? You dreaming, fool! Where you at, dog? Wake up and talk to me, Kory."

Opening my eyes, I hear Wayne shouting and shaking me. I respond,

"Wayne, I got a lot on my mind. Kara has got me all messed up."

Wayne looked at me and shook his head. He's disappointed in me.

"The bed is soaking wet, Kory. Get you a shower and come eat breakfast. I'll put a pot of coffee on."

He turned and walked away. I got out of bed and into the shower. Wayne let me borrow some of his clothes.

* * * * *

Wayne Calls Kara

"Hello,"

"Hello, Kara, this is Wayne."

Kara responded,

"Hey, Wayne."

"Kara, Kory spent the night at my place last night. We got a football game this morning with the kids. It's part of our community service. The field is located behind Rose Stadium. Do you know where the Legacy Building is located?"

Kara hesitated and then replied.

"Isn't that the place where you do early voting?"

"Yeah, Kara, that's it. The field is on the back side of the building. Kory could use your support. He had a rough night. I'm sure you did, too. We all got problems, Kara, but I know Kory loves you and the girls."

Kara is crying.

"Yeah, I had a rough night, too, Wayne. Kory and I had a big blow up. We both did wrong. But I still love Kory. I'll be there."

Kara is still crying.

"Kara, the game starts at nine o'clock."

"Ok, Wayne. See you at nine o'clock."

* * * * *

Youth Football ShowDown

I check my cell phone and there is another text from Mr. Preacher. I look at Wayne.

"Wayne, did you get a text from Mr. Preacher?"

Wayne responded,

"Yeah, I read it last night."

The text read,

"The evil beings won't leave you alone. They are deep inside of your head. Now you're afraid because you thought that part of your life was over. Remnants from your past will tempt you in the future. Evil spirits know what you like and will present them randomly throughout the rest of your life. Life is a test, and no one is exempt from sin. For the rest of your life, stay prayed up. Get on your knees and humble yourself before God. If not, you will relapse and fall deeper into the pit that you recently climbed from."

"Ok, it's time for us to go."

Wayne has a worried look on his face. He's my cousin, and I know he cares for me.

"Kory, are you up for the game today?"

"Yeah man, I'm good. We're in the playoffs. Let's go. We can take my truck."

Toni looked unsure about the truck and replied.

"Why don't we take the car?"

Wayne agreed.

"Yeah, the car might have a little more room for three adults."

Shaking my head in agreeance,

"I guess the two of you are right. Let's take the car."

I jumped in the back seat of Wayne's old-school car. The music was bumping all the way to the football field. It's a wonder we didn't get pulled over by the police. Wayne parked, and we went looking for Coach Jeff.

"Kory, I got another pair of shoes in the trunk if you want to take off your cowboy boots."

In a hip kind of way, I told him,

"Wayne, it's the weekend. My gators only come off when I go to bed."

We both laughed. Wayne replied,

"Ok, baller."

"Coach Jeff, how are you doing?" Coach is not looking too good.

"Fellas, I'm not doing too good. But I didn't want to let the kids down. I'm shaking, sweating and running a temperature. Today, you guys are going to have to do most of the coaching. The kids know you, so they will listen to you. I will be here if you need me."

I look at Coach Jeff, and he is right.

"Coach, you look like you need to be home in bed."

He replied,

"That's the same thing my wife said. But I am committed to helping these kids develop into good men. Too many of our young, black boys don't have good role models in their lives. Somebody needs to stand up for these kids. That's what I do."

I looked at Coach Jeff with tears in my eyes.

"Coach it is an honor to work with you. Me and Wayne won't let you down."

Wayne responded,

"Now, I understand why Mr. Preacher sent us to you. He knew you would be a positive influence for the both of us."

I nodded in agreeance with Wayne.

"Exactly, Wayne. Let's do this."

Talking louder,

"Let's do this, yeah! Let's play some football. Yeah!"

Everyone is cheering.

The whistle blows, and the game starts. We get the ball for the first series of plays. Me and Wayne alternate on calling plays. I called the first play.

"I Left 43 Lead on 2."

The first play from scrimmage we gain fifteen yards. The crowd is cheering.

"Your turn, Wayne."

Wayne calls the play.

"Power sweep right."

We gain another twenty yards. The crowd cheers again.

"Kory, I think we got the hang of this."

"Ok, I got another one, Wayne. I Right X Slant Pass."

We throw our first pass of the game and get a touchdown. The crowd goes wild. Wayne takes his cell phone out.

"Kory, I got Jerry Jones on the phone. He wants to talk to you."

Wayne and I are laughing and having a good time.

The opposing team gets the ball. They run several plays, and they do pretty good.

"Pass, cover the pass. Good hit. Oh, my goodness somebody got hurt, Wayne. Let's check it out."

All the coaches from both teams run to check on the kid from the opposing team. Coach Jeff was the first one there.

"Are you alright, son?"

I bend on one knee and make sure the kid is all right. We help him up and his father comes over. His father tells him,

"Shake it off, and don't cry. I ain't raising no punks."

The kid got up and went back to the huddle. Wayne got our team to huddle up. Coach Jeff talks to the kid's father.

"Hey, man. I know he's your son. And I know you want him to grow into a good man. But that's no way to talk to him. We all feel pain."

The father responded,

"He's my son, and I will raise him the way I want to."

Coaches from both teams are standing near. Coach Jeff couldn't let it go.

"I know he's your son, but it doesn't hurt to show a little love. Hell, we all feel pain. But that doesn't make us punks."

The father responded again.

"Shut up, you don't tell me nothing about my boy."

He made a motion toward Coach Jeff, and coaches from both teams grabbed him.

My baby girls were standing near. They ran up to me and hugged me. Kara hugged me, too. The kids father started to walk away until he saw Kara. He turned around slowly and took a good look at my family. Then he looked down at my boots.

"Nice boots Coach."

In a sarcastic way I replied,

"Thanks." As he walked away Kara whispered in my ear.

"That's Wolf Dog, Big Tilley's younger brother. His little girl is in Kelsi's gymnastics class."

Speaking softly to Kara,

"Kara, he just put two and two together. I haven't worn these boots since that night."

Kara knew the night I was talking about. Neither one of us wanted to speak the truth in front of the girls.

"Kara, keep an eye on him."

Wayne called the next play, and we talked.

"Kory, what's going on?"

I explained,

"Big Tilley's younger brother, Wolf Dog, is here. We need to keep an eye on him. That was his son that got hurt."

Wayne eyed him down.

"Yeah, I recognize him. I owe him an ass whooping. He's looking at us. Dang, another text from Mr. Preacher.

"Fate and Free Will. What the hell is that, Kory?"

Reading my text, I answered Wayne.

"I don't want to think about it right now. Hold up, Wayne, my phone is ringing. Hello."

Kory, I am taking the girls to mama's house, and I will be back."

"It's Kara, Wayne."

"Ok, Kara, watch your back."

"Ok, Kory, I will. Bye."

Our team ran another series of plays, and a group of thugs began to gather on the sideline.

"Wayne, I think we need to leave this place with the quickness."

Wayne and I are standing on the 50 yard line looking at each other.

"Kory, I think you are right. The only problem is the thugs are between us and my car."

The whistle blows. The game is over.

"Ok, Wayne let's walk to the opposite end of the field and walk around the block.

Pow, boom, bang, boom, bang, pow, bang, pow, boom. Everyone is running. Coach Jeff is trying to make sure all the kids are safe.

"Run, Wayne! They're shooting at us. Run toward the goal post and around the building!"

As we run and dodge bullets, we fall on the ground. Bullets are hitting the ground around us. We are low crawling like soldiers to keep from getting shot. We get up again and start running. A car is coming from around the building towards us. "Kory, damn, they got us. We're dead!"

"No, Wayne, they're too far away. They can't hit us. Get back on the ground."

Pow, pow, pow, bang, bang, boom, boom, the shots continue.

I take a moment to talk to God. 'Lord, is this it for me and Wayne? We have done a lot of things together. We tried to change, but I guess we didn't change fast enough. Now, that I think of it, you give us free will to live our lives the way we want to. But if we live our lives doing things that are harmful, we will go to an early grave. Thank you for the time that you gave me and Wayne. Looks like today is our last day.'

"They're coming from the other way, Kory. Ohhh, shit."

I stopped praying and looked up. The vehicle is driving on the field. The vehicle is coming toward me and Wayne at a high rate of speed. It stops right before it runs over the both of us. They are going to kill us slow and make us suffer.

I hear a loud scream as the bullets land around us.

"Kory, Kory, please don't be dead!"

The Calvary has arrived. It's Kara.

"Kory, the guns are in the trunk."

Wayne and I both grab weapons.

"Wayne, let's do this!"

We bumped fists with blood in our eyes.

"Kory, it's about to be on."

Wolf and his boys walk out on the football field. There is about 25 yards in between us. Wolf spoke,

"They tell me you're the bastard that killed my brother."

I answered.

"Yeah, I'm the bastard who killed your fat-ass brother."

He replied,

"Sounds like a confession."

I replied,

"Well, I got just one question for you, Wolf Puppy."

Wolf flexed his muscles and is mad as hell.

"And what might that question be, Alligator Boots?"

I answered,

"What do you want on your tombstone?"

He responded,

"You son of a ..."

pow, pow, pow, bang, bang, tat-tat-tat, tat-tat-tat, boom, boom. I charged shooting two automatic weapons at the same time. Wayne was screaming.

"Kory, what the hell are you doing?"

I screamed back at him.

"I got to finish this, Wayne! This is the last time. Lord don't leave me."

Tat-tat-tat, boom, boom, pow, pow, bang, bang, tat-tat-tat, tat-tat-tat.

When the last one of Wolf's men fell, I stopped shooting. Wayne was right by my side every step of the way.

"Kory, got damn it. Oh no!"

I looked at Wayne. He was looking behind us. With a frightening look on his face, he spoke in a loud voice.

"Kara got shot, Kory!"

Kara is lying on the ground next to the car. Running to Kara, I grab her and put her in the back seat of the car. Her body is limp. Don't leave me, Kara. She opens her eyes.

"Kory, I am sorry for doing wrong."

"I am sorry, too, Kara. The biggest problem in our marriage is me. My lifestyle pushed you in the wrong direction. Please, forgive me? I love you."

Kara's eyes closed. I shouted to Wayne.

"Get to the hospital as quick as you can!"

Holding her close to me, I prayed all the way to the hospital.

"Hold on, Kara".

My little Bonnie Parker is struggling for her life.

* * * * *

Church Business Meeting

There were no charges filed against us. Wolf Dog's gang was implicated in the murders of several people. Witnesses to the shooting corroborated our story. Dead men tell no lies. It is by the grace of God that we are alive and not in prison. Wayne and I went to see Mr. Preacher. We stopped by the church that he attends. They were having a business meeting. The members were involved in an intense argument. No one noticed that Wayne and I had walked in. We sat in the back of the church. A microphone stands in the middle aisle next to the front pew.

"Brother Pastor."

"Yes, Sister Tolbert."

"My family has been decorating this church for a long time. Every holiday we make this church look beautiful. God looks down on us and cries tears of joy."

Her family cheered and shouted amen. Another sister from a rival family pushed her way to the microphone.

"Brother Pastor.

"Yes, Sister Simpson."

"Every holiday, we have to cry through the same damn sorry decorations. I and many others in this church are sick and tired of the same people having too much authority."

Sister Tolbert took offense to what Sister Simpson said. Sister Tolbert replied.

"If you don't like the decorations, go your no singing-ass somewhere else. The choir will sound a whole lot better without your billy-goat voice."

Then, she made a sound like a goat. Sister Simpson took offense to the remarks made by Sister Tolbert. She pushed her way back to the microphone.

"I know one thing. Your husband likes the way I sing."

The fight jumped off. I turned to Wayne,

"I have never heard people in church argue over church decorations."

The fight was family against family. Mr. Preacher walked up to the podium. He motioned to the lady usher who was standing next to the deacon's pew. He spoke in a loud voice, so everyone could hear him.

"Bring me a rum and coke."

The church silenced. Mouths were hanging open. He continued.

"Oh, this is not a night club? Look at all the fighting and cussing going on in this church. Are you sure this is not a night club? For generations, the same families have attended this church. Generation after generation, you have not learned a thing. You have yet to change, and I do not see any growth among you. What are you teaching your children? Next Sunday, do not come to church. Stay at home and watch the Cowboys."

"Here is a secret. The best thing you can do is develop a personal relationship with God. Then, ask God why you were born in the first place ... Where is that drink, I ordered?"

The usher brought Mr. Preacher the drink he ordered. He tasted the drink. The drink took his breath away.

"Well, this bad boy is stout."

He held the drink up so the church could see it.

"How do you get a rum and coke in church?"

Somebody in the congregation shouted,

"Jesus, Jesus, Jesus."

Mr. Preacher responded.

"That's the problem. It's time to learn something else. It's time to preach a new way. All you need is God. God is real. Open your mind, do some research and stay woke."

"I will be starting my own church. The Church of the Truth will be opening soon."

The pastor of the church pushed himself in front of Mr. Preacher. He looked at Mr. Preacher as he talked.

"Excuse yourself from this church and never return. Get out!"

Mr. Preacher left the building.

Wayne and I ran outside to catch up with Mr. Preacher.

"Mr. Preacher, Mr. Preacher."

He stopped to talk to us before getting in his car.

"Fellas, how are the both of you doing?

We responded,

"We are fine, Mr. Preacher. Are you ok?

He responded.

"Yeah, fellas I'm just fine. I feel like I just walked across the stage and received my doctorate degree. What happened inside has been a long time coming.

Let me tell you guys something. If you don't seek your gift, you will find yourself back in the streets again. Next time, you may not live to tell the story. Go home and get on your knees. Ask God these words. 'Lord, what is my gift?' You will be surprised at the answer you get. God will show you your gift. Then your gift needs development. Find someone who is willing to help you. You need a good teacher."

Looking up in the sky and scratching my head, I thought for a moment.

"Mr. Preacher, I think I know what my gift is. I just didn't know it was a gift."

Wayne had a confused look on his face.

"I don't know what my gift is, Mr. Preacher. I don't have a clue."

Mr. Preacher got in his car and rolled down the window.

"Fellas, I got to go before the police show up."

We all laughed. I told him with tears in my eyes.

"I can't find the words to thank you enough, Mr. Preacher. But thanks anyway."

He drove away. Wayne and I were leaving as the police were driving into the parking lot. For the next nine months, we continued our community service.

* * * * *

The Wedding Theme
(Reflections of our Lives)

Everyone is smiling and waiting for the wedding couple. All the single girls are holding on to the single guys hoping they will be next. Seeing Alicia and Kelsi really makes me happy, and I'm trying not to get emotional. But I feel the tears coming. Both of my girls are cheerfully smiling as the wedding songs anoint the guests.

The groom is dressed in black-and white-striped clothing. Smith County Jail is written on the back of his shirt. Unlike most weddings, the groom stood in the foyer of the church. He walked slowly down the aisle. The lights are dim to set the mood. The wedding attendees closest to the front door are dressed like thugs, gangsters and prostitutes. Some of them displayed fake weapons. They looked like a lost generation. Others pretended to use drugs passing fake cigarettes back and forth to one another.

Halfway to the alter stands a huge tunnel. The groom stands and waits for his bride. The bride enters the church. She stands at the front door of the church, so everyone can see her. She is dressed in a dingy miniskirt that shows her red and brown underwear. She looks like a street walker. The father of the bride walks hand-in-hand with the bride. At the entrance of the tunnel, he gave her to the groom.

The bride and groom enter the tunnel of darkness. There is a bright light at the other end of the tunnel. Coming out of the tunnel, the bride and groom have changed clothes. Standing in the light the two of them smile at each other. They walk toward the altar.

The bridesmaids are beautiful, crying with tears and smiles. The groomsman stands tall and fly. Mr. Preacher stands underneath the trellis with Bible in hand. There isn't a dry eye in the house.

Vows exchange, and the bride and groom kiss. The bride and groom turn around and face the audience. Mr. Preacher presents the new couple. The tunnel is removed, and the new couple exits the church.

I open the door to the limousine. The bridesmaids hold the bride's dress off the ground. They help her get in the car and leave room for the groom.

Wayne and I have a brief conversation while the bridesmaids work on placing the dress.

"Kory, I know you've been working on your newly found gift. I talked to the guy who repaired your house after you wrecked your truck."

I paused for a moment to think.

"Oh, you're talking about the Mr. Hammond."

Wayne acknowledged, yes.

"Not only did I hire Mr. Hammond, but I also hired Pop's Construction Company. I had two contractors working at the same time. Kory, when you see it, I think you will like it."

Feeling grateful, I tried to hold it together.

"Wayne, you are my brother and closest friend. We have been through a lot together. You have always had my back. Wherever you are on this earth, I will be there for you."

We embraced. The bride said,

"Let's go, husband."

Wayne got in the car. He rolled the window down.

"Toni, I wish you and Wayne a lifetime of happiness."

She smiles.

"Thanks, Kory. Take care of my friend. You know she got your back."

I nodded,

"Ok."

As I walk toward Kara's new SUV, I see my baby girls in the back seat. Their smiles radiate a joyful glow. My little Bonnie Parker is seated in the front passenger seat. Her wounds have not healed yet. A bullet hit one of her bones, and it will take longer for her to fully recover. She is bandaged from her shoulder, down her back and around her waist. Pillows are placed around her to keep her comfortable. I crank up the car and look at her.

"How do you feel?"

She replied,

"I'm doing much better. The kids want to see our new family business."

The girls agree.

"Yeah, Daddy, let's go see the new family business."

I looked at their smiling faces.

"Well, since you twisted my arm, I guess so."

Alisha starts singing along with the radio. We drive up Houston Street and turn left on Glenwood.

Driving up Glenwood brings back a lot of childhood memories. The veterinarian on the right side of the street was where my dad and I took my puppy. My puppy used to climb upon the table and jump off. I caught him in the air, and we both rolled around on the floor. He licked me in my face.

Across the street was Wright's Place. They always had good food. My dad and I tried everything on the menu. Everything was good. Across the street from Wright's Place was the baseball field where I hit my first homerun. The ball didn't go over the fence, but I had enough speed to run around the bases before they could throw me out. Man, I had a great childhood. I miss my dad. I stopped for the red light at Gentry Parkway. Across the street sitting on the corner is my new family business. "The Pharaoh of Barbeque" is a great name if I must say so myself.

We drove into the parking lot and parked across several parking spaces. Today is a nice warm September day. The landscape is beautiful. The lantana shrubs are covered with butterflies and hummingbirds. Kelsi, the butterfly queen, is having the time of her life. I removed two lawn chairs from the back of the SUV. I helped Kara get seated comfortably. The two of us sat there like two old people watching our girls run and play. Kelsi ran to me.

"Daddy, look!"

I answered,

"Look at what, baby?"

She explained,

"The butterflies are all over you. They are even on your head. God forgives you Daddy."

We all had a group hug.

I wasted too much time living a lifestyle that wasn't meant for me to live. I gained absolutely nothing. But I almost lost everything that is important in life. It took a long time for me to reach this point. It's by the grace of God that my journey didn't end in death. My change is accredited to the Almighty. When he changed me, he blessed me. Maybe, I will write a book and share my story with the world. Maybe not.

Going Through is a journey that will lead you to your epiphany. You will discover your gift and understand the reason that you were born.

Wait a minute. I need to make one more phone call.

"Hello."

"Hey, Mr. Preacher. This is Kory. I got to ask you a question."

"What is the question, Kory?"

"Who is Stickman?"

Mr. Preacher laughed.

"Kory, Stickman is a description of someone living their life pretending to be someone else. Live the life that God has for you. Discover your gift. Develop your gift and use your gift. Then you will find happiness, success and good fortune."

"Thanks, Mr. Preacher … I just started living my life."